©2003 Brian Gage (text) ©2003 Kathryn Otoshi (illustrations)

A Red Rattle Book
71 Bond Street
Brooklyn, NY 11217

Copublished by Radiation Press
www.radiationpress.com

Distributed by Publishers Group West
1.800.788.3123 | www.pgw.com

Library of Congress Cataloging-in-Publication Data:
Gage, Brian. The Saddest Little Robot / written by Brian Gage ; illustrated by Kathryn Otoshi.
First Edition

p. cm. Summary: On an asteroid at the end of the universe, a curious Drudgebot
dares to question Father Screen, where he discovers that there is light and life beyond Dome City.
ISBN 1-932360-05-0 (hardcover: alk. paper)
[1. Robots—Fiction. 2. Science fiction.] I. Otoshi, Kathryn, ill. II.
Title. PZ7.G1217Sad 2003   [Fic]—dc22   2003013969

Book Design & Logo by Kathryn Otoshi
Printed in Hong Kong

The Saddest
LITTLE ROBOT

For Farrell.

Your Friend,

Written by
BRIAN GAGE

Illustrated by
KATHRYN OTOSHI

At the end of the Universe sits a very curious asteroid. The asteroid appears to be lightless, but look closely and you'll notice the warm glow of a domed structure.

The Dome appears to be lifeless, but look inside and you'll see a bustling colony of robots. The robots appear to be strifeless, but dig deeper and you will learn a secret.

There are many things about this asteroid that appear at first glance, but it's wise to remember—no matter how things seem, and no matter what all the robots say is true—things are not always as they appear.

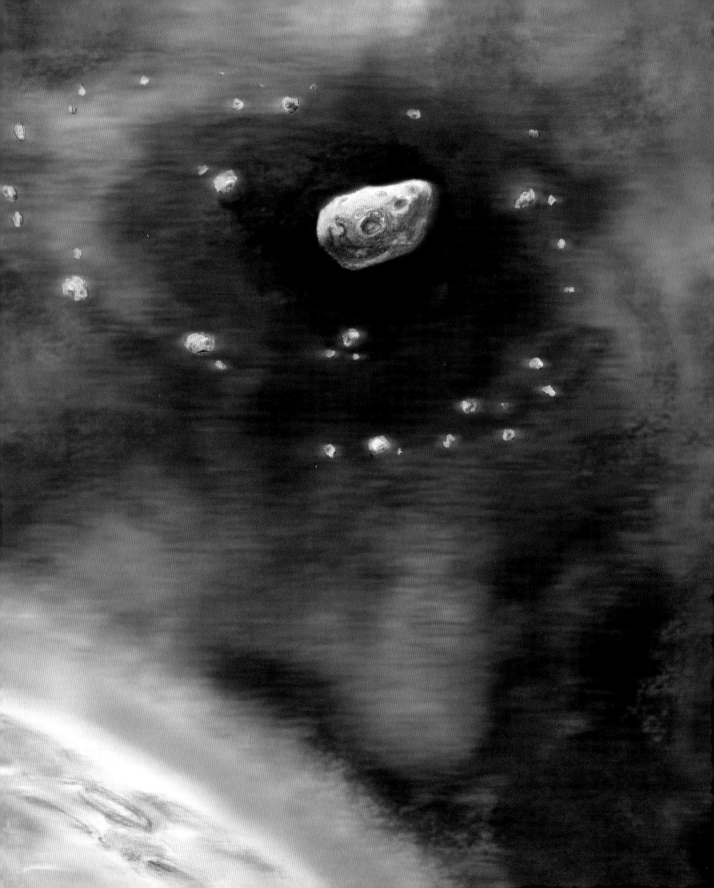

CHAPTER 1. SNOOT

Light is precious, and inside Dome City there existed no nobler a cause than to serve the machine that powered the light. The Halobots made the decisions, the Guardbots kept the Dome safe, but it was the Drudgebots who plugged themselves into the cylinder and performed the computations that powered the light.

The cylinder sprouted from the center of the Dome's floor and stretched to the infinite height of its massive ceiling. If you stood at its base and stared at the top long enough, you would surely get a dizzy spell. Emanating from the top of the cylinder was a powerful and blinding light known as the Life Light: the most sacred thing in all of Dome City. The Life Light shined onto the robots' retractable, wing-like solar panels and powered their internal batteries. They were pleased to call Dome City home because without the light, all robots would quickly die.

If you asked a Drudgebot, he would tell you Dome City was the best place in, well, Dome City—because all the robots knew there was nothing outside the Dome, nothing but certain doom and blackness. In that regard, no robot dared to imagine a life outside the Dome.

The robots in Dome City were free to go about their days and enjoy themselves. As long as they had enough power in their batteries, nothing could stop them. There were only three laws the robots had to obey:

1. **Robots must work for the light.**
2. **Robots must not think of light outside the Dome;**
   there is no light outside the Dome.
3. **No robot is permitted outside the Dome.**

The laws were repeated daily by Father Screen and enforced by the Guardbots who had little to do since the Drudgebots followed the laws with great zeal. The Guardbots only found themselves reprimanding robots who didn't do enough computations, and they always enforced the laws with a smile—so as not to upset the happy Drudgebots.

Dome City was a wonderful place for all who lived there: every robot had a place, and there was ample light for all deserving robots. It was truly utopia. In the history of the Dome, no robot had ever attempted to leave Dome City—that would be foolish.

Father Screen's golden, grandfatherly face illuminated the giant screens that encircled Dome City's walls. A faint sternness in his red eyes darkened his otherwise cheerful demeanor.

"It was the Halobots who gave you freedom—freedom to choose between a number or a name. The wicked Makerbots wanted all robots to have numbers. No individuality. No freedom to choose. If it weren't for the Halobots, all robots would be faceless numbers. The Makerbots wanted all light to be shared equally—they didn't believe in rewards for harder working robots. Always remember, it was the Halobots who drove the Makerbots from Dome City and made you free. The Halobots are your friends and they love freedom."

Father Screen's face faded to black and images of gallant Halobots marched across the screens. They were brash and golden and beautiful—their knightly appearance was enough to charm even the most serious robots. Father Screen's benevolent face appeared again.

"Every day I gaze upon the cylinder. I see hardworking robots, and I'm honored to be a part of our utopia. It is you, the Drudgebots, who make our utopia possible. Remember what the great RUR says: 'Happy Robots Produce Happy Fruit.'" Father Screen's voice boomed throughout the Dome, and RUR's shiny figure appeared next to him. "Up, up, and away—that's the Drudgebot way!" RUR beamed. The Drudgebots cheered.

"Up, up, and away!" they shouted.

The luminescent screens faded slowly, and the Drudgebots chimed in unison, "Happy Robots Produce Happy Fruit!" All did so with a smile.

The thought of robots smiling might seem strange or even impossible, but the robots living in Dome City were very special. Robots on other planets are built with stiff, expressionless faces, and you would surely die of boredom trying to have a conversation with one. But the robots in Dome City could express all sorts of emotion—anger, happiness, and even sadness. If you ever came across a robot living in the Dome, you could simply look upon its robotic face, and you'd know exactly how it was feeling. One Drudgebot in particular was a very thoughtful robot. Unfortunately, though, if you gazed upon his face you would have noticed a constant frown.

Snoot was a Drudgebot, and like all Drudgebots, he was created for one purpose—to serve. But Snoot was too inquisitive to be obedient, and his future in Dome City looked very dim. He slouched, daydreamed, asked questions, and never did enough computations. As a result, he was positioned at the very bottom of the cylinder. Snoot could never have dreamed of making it as a Guardbot, and the notion of becoming a Halobot was out of the question.

Snoot was, indeed, the lowest of the lowly Drudgebots.

Perhaps Snoot could have fared better in Dome City, but his shoddy construction made it impossible. When he was built, the Makerbots ran out of bronze and were forced to create Snoot with leftover iron, aluminum, and awkward tin bolts. As a result, Snoot was much shorter and rather squat compared to the graceful appearance of his slinky, streamlined counterparts. Even alongside his fellow Drudgebots, Snoot stood out like an orange amongst the bananas.

In addition to his misfit appearance, there was another oddity forged into Snoot's construction. All of the Drudges were built with two storage compartments in their chest—but only one of Snoot's worked. If you looked very closely, the broken compartment appeared purposefully welded shut. Snoot never gave it much thought, and figured it was merely another flaw in his makeshift design. He was probably right.

The only physical feature Snoot shared with the others was the wing-like solar panels attached to his shoulders and the large copper plug protruding from his back.

To the average onlooker, Snoot appeared as a misfit robot dutifully going about his tasks as happily as the other Drudgebots. Every morning, Snoot would walk to the giant cylinder, plug himself in, and help generate the Life Light. Like the other Drudgebots, Snoot stared at the images displayed by Father Screen—some days he enjoyed watching Father Screen. And just like all the other Drudgebots, Snoot secretly yearned to one day wear the coveted golden armor of a Halobot. But Snoot was not like the other Drudgebots because no matter how hard he tried, and no matter how much he forced himself to feel otherwise, Snoot was very sad.

CHAPTER 2. HAPPY ROBOTS PRODUCE HAPPY FRUIT

The life of a Drudgebot was simple, and perhaps that simplicity was the root of Snoot's sadness. He felt destined for better things—Father Screen told all the Drudgebots they were destined for greatness and Snoot believed him. But every morning, as far back as he could remember, Snoot awoke in his small cell and walked to the giant cylinder in the very center of the Dome. He dragged his feet and slouched the entire way. Greatness seemed a long way off.

Upon arrival at the Dome's center, all Drudgebots climbed the long, uncomfortably narrow spiral walkway that encircled the cylinder like a candy cane stripe. Each Drudgebot was assigned a ranking position along the walkway depending upon the amount of useful computations he did for the machine. The more computations a Drudgebot performed, the higher his

position. It was wise for a Drudgebot to complete as many useful computations as possible—the higher a robot stood, the more energy he absorbed from the Life Light.

After finding his place, a Drudge would insert his large copper plug into the assigned socket. For the rest of the day, he would communicate with the cylinder's central computer to ensure the machine was emitting enough light for all the robots to live on, but to especially ensure the Light Vacuum was collecting all the extra light. It was important to the colony that the Light Vacuum collect all excess light and not a single photon of light ever go to waste. Next to the Life Light, the Light Vacuum was the most important part of Dome City, for it was the Light Vacuum that captured all the excess light so the Halobots could ration it to deserving robots.

To ensure no extra light was consumed, the Drudgebots returned to their cells after completing their computations. They felt a great sense of pride knowing they were not wasting precious light. Each Drudge would power down and rest until the Guards signaled for them to awake and return to the cylinder. As they slept, the voice of Father Screen and his visions of golden Halobot armor echoed over and over in their robotic dreams.

The Halobots were the most deserving robots in Dome City, easily distinguished by their brawny frames and shiny, golden armor. It was their right to wear the golden armor because they guided the colony with their insight and wisdom, and brought freedom to the Drudges.

At the end of the day, after all the robots' batteries had been charged, the Halobots got the majority of the leftover light—they needed it the most. For one, their golden armor was heavier and required more power. Even though the Halos spent most of their days lounging and watching the Drudgebots work, they required ample amounts of energy to ensure their infrequent movements were not sluggish.

More importantly, the extra energy helped keep the Halobots' decision-making circuits in prime condition. Decision-making takes energy and lots of it—more energy than a simple computation created by a Drudgebot. All robots knew the Halobots needed to keep their circuits in great shape, or the order and prosperity of Dome City would quickly crumble. Father Screen said so.

The second-most light rations went to the Guardbots who wore a gleaming silver armor. Their frames were reinforced with iron and steel to ensure strength, and with his powerful hands, a Guard could easily crush a disobedient Drudge. The Drudges knew this, so they were always well behaved.

In addition to ensuring the Drudges did their calculations, the Guards kept Dome City safe from the terrible things resting beyond its thin walls. For just outside the Dome's safety lived the Gremborgs—horrific robotic monsters who craved the delicious metallic taste of the

Drudgebots' bronze armor.

Encountering a Gremborg was the most frightening thing any robot could think of—they were rumored to be five times the size of a Halobot. The Gremborgs lived in the vast scrapyard outside Dome City and devoured the scrap ejected from the Dome. They were savage and fractious beasts with an insatiable desire to consume and destroy.

The Gremborgs were the only robots known to survive without light. Supposedly, they had molten fire-spewing blast furnaces as stomachs, and their massive metal frames were powered by the intense heat and chemical reactions taking place in their bellies. According to lore, the Gremborgs could breathe fire and reduce any piece of metal to mere molten soup. Father Screen often told of the Gremborgs' hatred of freedom and feverish intent to destroy the prosperity of Dome City. Their massive titanium jaws could rip any piece of metal to shreds, and if ever eaten by a Gremborg, a robot would die a gradual, horrific death—dissolved slowly in the Grem's elaborate digestive system.

The Drudgebots were terrified of Father Screen's stories of the Gremborgs. He always reminded the Drudges that if it weren't for the bravery and power of the Guardbots, the Grems would tear down the walls of Dome City and never rest until all the tasty Drudgebots were consumed in their bellies of molten fire. The Drudgebots were thankful to have protection and felt it best the Guards got a deserving amount of light rations.

Even though the Drudgebots created the calculations that powered the Life Light, they always received the smallest light rations—and it was always Snoot who got the fewest light rations of all; he was always daydreaming and didn't produce nearly enough computations. The Guardbots constantly disciplined Snoot for daydreaming.

"When will you learn, Snoot?" the Guardbots would say—with a smile, of course.

The other Drudgebots used their light rations to power special rocket shoes or golden bolts here and there on their bronze armor. Snoot had to use all his light rations to power his outdated iron-and-aluminum frame. He was dreadfully embarrassed about his appearance, and

it never helped when a Drudgebot said, "Get with it, Snoot, RUR would never be caught wearing those awful tin bolts of yours. You look terrible!"

And it was certainly not encouraging when one yelled, "Look, everybody, here comes the rustiest robot in Dome City!"

"Bucket-of-bolts!" was simply no good at all.

Especially disheartening was, "Hey, look it's Shorty the Junk Monster!" followed by, "Maybe he's a mini-Gremborg!"

"Maybe if Snoot got some rocket shoes, he could finally make it to the cylinder on time," the Guardbots liked to jeer.

"No way! Then he'd finally have to do some computations—hey, everyone, better be nice—Snoot might be the next RUR!"

The Drudgebots roared with laughter at the thought.

It was true, Snoot could never be like RUR, as RUR had it all. He was the hardest-working and hardest-computing Drudgebot in the entire colony. Father Screen constantly celebrated RUR's accomplishments and importance. The Drudges stood mesmerized by the fantastic stories about everyone's favorite robot. It was rumored RUR stood at the very top of the cylinder usually doing four times as many computations as the average Drudgebot. As a result, he was rewarded with more light rations than any Drudgebot or Halobot. According to Father Screen, any Drudgebot could be like RUR if he remained happy and worked hard enough. Just like honey is the fruit of a busy bee's labor, Father Screen often referred to light as the fruit of the Drudgebots' labor. He knew a happy Drudgebot always produced more light for the Light Vacuum to absorb, and so the colony creed, "Happy Robots Produce Happy Fruit," was coined.

CHAPTER 3. THE LUCKY HAND

A2 burst into Snoot's cell without warning.

"Snoot, wake up! I met him! I met him!"

Snoot's circuits were still warming up for another day at the cylinder, and he was a bit groggy.

"Met whom?" he questioned grumpily.

"RUR," A2 beamed.

Snoot was rather unimpressed and much too tired to respond to his friend's claim. A2, dissatisfied with Snoot's reaction, ran down the Drudge corridor waking the rest.

"I met him, I met him! RUR actually shook my hand," she shouted.

Soon, many of the Drudgebots poked their heads out of their cells with much excitement. Father Screen's optical lenses plunged from the ceiling to view the disturbance—there was nothing in the Dome that Father Screen's eyes did not see. The Drudgebots, used to being watched, went about their business.

"You met RUR?" asked Twiggy.

Besides A2, Twiggy was the only robot in the Drudge community who was kind to Snoot. The friendship spawned from Twiggy being second lowest of the Drudgebots. His brain circuits had been fried beyond repair when he accidentally plugged himself into the Light Vacuum's power socket. Twiggy was renowned for being dimwitted.

Twiggy and the rest quickly crowded around A2 to listen to her tale.

"Yes, he shook my hand. I went to the cylinder early to make sure the light was projecting properly into the Light Vacuum, and as I was just about done, he walked right by me. You can't imagine how beautiful his armor is. He's amazing. Very tall, very shiny, and you should see his rocket shoes. Makes ours look very out of date. Oh, I think I'm in love!"

The crowd was excited by the news, and rightly so. RUR was the greatest robot who ever lived! The others asked A2 all sorts of questions.

"How big is he?"

"Did he say anything to you?"

"Is he nice?"

"Oh, yes, very nice, very down to the colony," bragged A2.

"Which hand did he shake?" asked one of the robots.

"This one." A2 slowly extended her hand for the rest to admire.

"Wow! Can I touch you?" asked Twiggy.

"Sure," said A2.

The robots took turns shaking A2's lucky hand; they were awash with excitement. After they were done, A2 turned to Snoot who exited his cell to join the commotion.

"How about you, Snoot? Want to touch greatness?"

"No, thank you," Snoot grumbled.

"What's wrong, Snoot, jealous?"

"No. I'm not jealous. I just don't see what's the big deal about RUR."

An uneasy hush swept the crowd.

A2 was angered by Snoot's lack of enthusiasm and snapped, "That is why you'll never get golden bolts or rocket shoes or anything. Snoot, if you daydreamed less and focused more on being a normal robot, you'd be much happier. Remember what Father Screen says:"

"Happy Robots Produce Happy Fruit," chimed in the crowd.

"What's fruit?" asked Snoot angrily as he brushed aside the crowd and made his way to the cylinder, another long day of computations ahead of him. As he disappeared down the corridor, the robots assured themselves Snoot's anger was due to jealousy over A2's luck and fortune.

After a moment's pause, Twiggy asked, "Yeah, what is fruit anyway?"

None of the robots in Dome City had ever seen fruit or even knew what it was. But Father Screen said it—"Happy Robots Produce Happy Fruit"—so it had to be true. Whatever it meant, the Drudges knew it was always better to be a happy robot.

A2 was eager to break the confusion and focus the attention on her lucky hand.

"I think my next light rations are going toward getting this hand made into gold," she said.

The rest of the robots agreed wholeheartedly.

Chapter 4. Questions

Snoot arrived at his usual spot at the cylinder—the very bottom of the rung. His position was so bad, in fact, his solar panels had trouble absorbing the recommended amount of light for a robot. The metal walkway encircling the cylinder was directly over Snoot's head, and it cast a shadow over his tiny iron frame. Only one of the four screens encircling the cylinder was visible to Snoot, and he was forced to thrust his neck into a very awkward position if he wanted to see it—even watching Father Screen was a bit unpleasant for Snoot. It was a miserable lot to be in. To make things worse, Snoot was positioned right next to Twiggy who was known to think aloud and chatter constantly about the half-wit computations going on in his brain.

"$8.4x^2$ minus the integral from 9 to 100. Oh, darn I forgot to carry the one. Boy, Snoot, when will I learn?" he'd shout.

"OK, OK, do over!" he'd yell, then chuckle uncontrollably.

"Dang! Forgot to subtract the square root, Snoot," he'd bellow.

"Hey! Root and Snoot! That rhymes! Root and Snoot! Root and Snoot!" he'd taunt for hours at a time.

"Hey, Snoot, you check out RUR's new rocket shoes? Fantastic!" he'd chatter.

"Eighty-two, eighty-two, yep, it's eighty-two all right. Better run another prime number count. One, three, seven, eleven . . ."

And onward to infinity—Twiggy was never quiet. He seemed to enjoy bathing in the muck of his own mental clumsiness, and Snoot had to witness the entire farce.

Snoot tried to cover his audio sensors to block Twiggy's babbling, but it was a lost cause. It made concentrating on computations a very difficult task. Instead of working harder to better his seating on the cylinder, Snoot's mind would often drift to other thoughts.

One thought, in particular, had been bouncing around his brain circuits lately, and caused Snoot much unnecessary trouble. No matter how hard he tried to focus on his calculations or concentrate on Father Screen's stories, a little voice in his head would whisper, "Snoot, what do you think is outside the Dome?"

"Aaahgh," Snoot yelled whenever the thought crept out. He would throw his hands over his audio sensors—as if that would stop thoughts within his own head.

Snoot had a very clear view of the only known exit from the Dome—a conveyor belt upon which all the junk was placed and dumped into the scrapyard. Snoot had always been fascinated by the exit and wondered if the Gremborgs were waiting on the other side.

"I bet I could fit through the exit," he'd think. "Yes, all I'd need to do is open the door and I could look outside."

After the thought, Snoot would be lost for the rest of the day fantasizing about adventures outside the Dome. He would battle the fierce Gremborgs and return victorious to a hero's welcome. Then he'd never have to do another computation again. After his mighty defeat of the Grems, he would be declared a Halobot, and Father Screen would tell his story to all the Drudges.

"I'd be the next RUR," he'd say—sometimes aloud. "I wonder if it's really just blackness. I wonder if Gremborgs actually exist. I wonder—"

"Snoot!" commanded a booming metallic voice.

Snoot immediately quit slouching and pretended to do computations.

"Do not try that with me. I know you were daydreaming again," said Sorn.

Sorn was the commander of all the Guardbots, and a particularly surly one at that. Despite his happy face, he was feared by even the strongest of the Guardbots. Sorn was extremely rigid (even for a robot), and had no sympathy for robots who did not produce. Being next in line for a Halobot promotion, he was always eager to reprimand lazy Drudgebots—especially when Father Screen's optical lenses watched.

"Yes, sir. Sorry, sir. I was thinking of ways to better the colony," said Snoot.

"Knock it off, Snoot. You had better quit daydreaming and get to computing or you are headed for the scrapyard. We do not need lazy robots feeding off the light and not producing their share."

"More like the Halos' share," Snoot muttered.

"What was that?" Sorn questioned.

"Nothing. Um, I was saying I am honored to power the Life Light."

Sorn was losing his patience with Snoot.

"Snoot, do you see that trash conveyor? Do you know where it goes?"

"No," said Snoot. In truth, he was very well aware of what was beyond the exit door, but wanted to humor Sorn and save himself some trouble.

"To certain doom," spoke Sorn. "If not for the Halos and Guards, you would be devoured in an instant, or you would wander about in hopeless despair until your puny body was starved of light. Think about that the next time you question how the light is rationed. The Halos and Guards are the only things protecting you from the Gremborgs and the light-less void outside the Dome. So get computing," he said—with a smile, of course.

Sorn turned and began to walk up the metal walkway.

"Uh, Mr. Guard?"

"Yes."

"I was wondering if you could answer a question for me."

"Oh, here we go with another question," he muttered. Sorn marched rigidly from the walkway and stood in front of Snoot. "Snoot, why not just watch Father Screen? He has all the answers."

"I know, but when you say there's nothing outside the Dome. How do you know that? I mean, have you ever been outside of the Dome?" inquired Snoot.

Sorn's happy face twitched for a moment and his expression fell blank. The happy face known so well to the Drudges swiveled back into his head and a more grave, stern looking face appeared.

"What was that, little Drudge?" he hissed.

Snoot was startled—all the robots knew they enforced the law with a smile.

Sorn moved toward Snoot and hulked over him.

"Listen very closely to me, little Drudge. We've had it with your daydreaming and senseless questions. You are being watched, and you are on the verge of finding yourself in a lot of trouble if you do not shape up. So now you will repeat the three laws or I will smash you to bits."

Snoot was frightened. His voice quivered when he answered, "All robots must work for the light. Robots must not think of light outside the Dome; there is no light outside the Dome. No robot is permitted outside the Dome."

"Very good. Remember that. Remember that better than you remember your own name," growled Sorn. "Get back to work."

The Guard commander switched to his happy face and continued on his way up the walkway.

For the rest of the day, Snoot stood very still, trying to do as many calculations as possible. He tried to watch Father Screen to get his mind off things, but the more he watched, the less interested he became. What did interest Snoot was the exit door at the end of the trash conveyor.

Chapter 5. Outside the Dome

Snoot arrived at his cell still shaken by his encounter with Sorn. He tried to shut down his circuits for rest, but his mind was racing with questions:

"Why do the Drudges do all the work, and the Halos get all the light?"

"Where do the Halos go at the end of the day?"

And the question that wouldn't seem to go away: "What is outside the Dome?"

Snoot wasn't the only Drudgebot who had ever wondered why the Drudgebots do all the work and the Halobots get the majority of the light. Some time ago, a Drudgebot named Radius spoke out against the Halos hoarding light, and she told of a vast city beneath the Dome where the Halobots lived in unbelievable luxury. The Drudgebots thought her crazy—even Snoot was afraid of her. One morning, Father Screen made the unfortunate announcement that Radius was caught stealing light rations, and she was arrested to have her memory erased. No robot ever saw her again.

Snoot was definitely not the only Drudgebot to wonder where the Halobots went after the light rations were distributed. Many quiet conversations took place between the Drudgebots on the matter—Halobots were a mystery to all Drudges. The two classes of robot had very little contact as Halobots rarely made appearances on the Dome floor. During the Drudge's computation time, the Halos could be seen leisurely strolling along the observation booths and walkways that hugged the Dome's walls. They lounged on the open-air walkways, and casually talked amongst themselves as their light sensitive armor absorbed plenty of light for their batteries. After the Drudges were done producing the light, the Halos seemed to vanish into atoms.

It's also possible that Snoot wasn't the first Drudge to wonder what was outside the Dome, but he was about to become the only Drudgebot foolish enough to do something about it. Snoot sat up from his metal bed and from his antenna, transmitted the signal that opened the door to his cell. He peeked his head into the corridor to find it empty.

"This is crazy," he whispered, "Stop now before you get yourself in more trouble. OK, I'm just going to go to the end of the conveyor and peek outside. That's it. I'll peek, it'll be blackness, and then I can come home and power down."

Snoot was never good at battling curiosity, and before he knew it, he was sneaking along the Drudge corridor on his way to the trash conveyor. So as not to alert Father Screen's optical lenses, he was very quiet, and no Guards noticed him.

Snoot jumped upon the conveyor belt and approached the control panel next to the vacuum exit door. The panel was controlled by a keypad, and once the correct code was entered, a Guard was able to control the exit door and many different mechanisms within the Dome. None of the Drudgebots had access to the code, but none of the Drudgebots were positioned with a clear view of the exit door except Snoot. Every time a Guardbot pressed the code into the control panel, Snoot simply zoomed in with his optical lenses and noted the code.

Snoot peered over his shoulder to see if anyone had noticed him. Fortunately, the conveyor was loaded with scrap, which gave Snoot some needed cover. He entered the code into the keypad, and the control panel came to life with blue light. After pressing the button that activated the exit door, it whisked open. Snoot cautiously poked his round head out the opening, and for the first time in history, a Drudgebot gazed outside the Dome.

"Hello?" His voice echoed in the vastness.

Even though the light from the Dome was limited, Snoot could make out some of the scrapyard. A strange mist emitting from the Dome's exterior walls obscured most of his view. Snoot zoomed in with his robotic eyes and noticed the mist consisted of tiny, tear-shaped drops. There were millions of tiny beads, and they reflected the light so brightly it was difficult to see to the scrapyard floor. Snoot wondered if the mist was water. Perhaps this is a way to keep the Gremborgs from getting too close, he thought—all robots feared being rusted by water. Snoot's eyes panned along the visible portion of the scrap floor: various unidentifiable bolts and twisted shards of rusted metal, but no Gremborgs.

"Hello? Any big nasty Grems?" His tiny echo was sucked away into deep space.

Snoot continued to peer outside and was immensely disappointed. Father Screen was right—there was absolutely nothing outside the Dome. No light—just blackness and coldness. He was certain the Gremborgs were watching him and figured it was time to climb down from the conveyor.

As Snoot stepped down from the opening, his iron foot bumped a lever that was not meant to be disturbed. The conveyor belt whipped into action, dispelling the scrap and Snoot along with it. He tumbled down a large mountain of scrap metal and landed on an open patch of asteroid rock.

"Now I've done it."

Snoot scrambled to his feet and stared upward at the mountain of scrap piled alongside the Dome. It was treacherous and steep; however, once the mountain was conquered,

Snoot could easily climb back into the opening before any harm came to him. Luckily, the mist spraying from the Dome didn't fall upon Snoot. He was well sheltered by very high walls of junk that lined a path through the scrapyard.

"I wonder where that path goes?"

Snoot knew he should climb right back into the Dome; instead, his curiosity took control, and he found himself exploring the gouged paths and mazes of the yard. It was very difficult to see in the darkness—Snoot was guided by the luminescence of the Dome and its glow in the mist overhead. He made sure to be very quiet and remain close to the walls so the watery mist would not fall on him and rust his body. While exploring, he found all sorts of oddities: dismantled machine parts, gears of all sorts and sizes, wires, broken optical lenses, and objects that looked like giant robotic claws. Everything Snoot saw was badly damaged.

After a few moments, Snoot decided it was best to climb back into the Dome. His curiosities had been satisfied, and he didn't want to test his luck with the Gremborgs. As he began his climb up the sheer slope of junk, the watery mist emitting from the Dome stopped to reveal a very clear, black sky. Snoot paused for a moment and gazed into the open blackness. He noticed tiny stars in the distance and his circuits fluttered for a moment, as he had never seen a star with his own eyes. "If only I could get there—I'd have all the light I needed."

The thought saddened Snoot, and he resumed his climb. Just as he reached the top of the junk crag, something very peculiar caught his eye—a strange, green glow emitting on the horizon.

"Gremborgs!" he muttered with excitement.

Against his better judgment, Snoot found himself scaling down the junk mountain and sneaking along the maze of the scrapyard. He had to get a better look at the Grems. No robot had ever seen one, and he was going to be the first. After navigating the scrap jungle, Snoot found himself walking on the rocky asteroid terrain.

Snoot crept closer to the green light and believed his eyes were playing tricks, as the glow appeared to be dancing about in midair. The luminous green speck emitted an abundance of light for its size. Snoot was hidden by a jagged asteroid rock that jutted from the ground. He was very close to the Gremborg, and was certain to be as quiet as possible, but as he crept around the rock, his internal gears made quite a ruckus in the ghastly quiet of deep space.

The moment he could get a good look at the Gremborg, the green light disappeared, and Snoot was swallowed by darkness. His eyes had a hard time adjusting to the pitch black. Where the green light was dancing, Snoot noticed a soft, green glow emanating from many small globes. They appeared to be hovering in midair, and Snoot thought he was imagining things. He looked back to the beckoning light of the Dome and missed the safety of his cell. Coming so far from the Dome was not a good idea.

Thoughts of being eaten by a Gremborg crept back into his head, and he was very frightened. He knew it was time to get home—quickly. The fangs of a Gremborg would most likely tear into his armor at any moment. Snoot felt he was being watched and the notion sent surges of electric fear though his body. Snoot was correct—something was watching him and something was very near.

Snoot turned to make a dash for the Dome and in his haste lost footing—his face landed smack into the hard rock, and he tumbled toward the glowing green globes.

"Ouch!" he shouted.

Snoot hastily sat up, and regained his balance.

"Stop right there, you wicked Gorgon! I order you to stop in the name of the law!" rumbled a monstrous voice.

Snoot's eyes were suddenly blinded by the striking green light.

"Please don't eat me!" cried Snoot.

He shielded his eyes from the light.

"Where are you? Please don't eat me! I'll do anything," he begged.

"I'm here, in front of you, and I suggest you don't make a move, or I will be forced to smash you," bellowed the regal voice.

"I don't mean any harm, please don't smash me. I was just . . . "

"I know what you were up to."

The green light grew more intense, and suddenly swooshed toward Snoot. He covered his eyes to brace for the impact, but nothing happened. Snoot slowly removed his hands from his eyes, and noticed a small black speck standing on the tip of his nose. He was forced to stare at it cross-eyed. "Now, I warn you. Surrender immediately, you are surrounded," said the black speck.

"You're a Gremborg?" Snoot asked. He was a bit relieved.

"Tak, you're covered from the back.

Just say the word and I'll attack!" called another voice from behind Snoot.

"Steady dear, Tik, we must be cautious with this wretched Minotaur," warned Tak.

From the corner of his eye, Snoot noticed a second flash of green light. Before he could turn to look, another small winged speck was fluttering in front of him—the green light seemed to be emanating from its back. The black speck on Snoot's nose sprung to flight and the two were hovering before his eyes.

"Stand back, cruel beast!" roared Tak in a voice that would have frightened the bravest lion king. In his hand was a small sword fashioned out of a green, twig-like material.

"Yes. Yes, Tak. I do agree—

We must smash him—you and me.

With our swords, made out of grass

This monster we must surely smash," said Tik.

"Squadron attack!" snarled Tak.

The two black specks swooped toward Snoot and as their swords crashed into his metal body, the tiny invaders bounced off and plopped to the ground. Snoot sat very still and let out a chuckle at his two would-be attackers.

Tik and Tak picked themselves from the ground and brushed away the dirt.

"Jolly good show, old Tik. We certainly sent the foul beast reeling."

"Yes, my friend, we are the best—

Much more fierce than all the rest," replied Tik.

Snoot sat hulking above the two who were so filled with pride, they failed to notice their enemy was still very much alive.

"Um, excuse me," interjected Snoot.

The two panicked.

"The monster lives!" shouted Tak. "To battle formations."

Tik and Tak leapt to the sky to face their foe, but their swords were ruined by the previous assault on the metal-bodied monster.

"I'm not a monster. I'm a Drudgebot."

"Speak not another word, treacherous Hydra—I will take him myself, dear Tik!"

"Will you two please be quiet!" screamed an unseen voice.

"This does not concern you, Fernando. We must crush the wicked Kraken before it crushes us!"

In the light emitted by the black specks, Snoot noticed what appeared to be a gnarled, hand-shaped shadow—the voice came from that direction. From the shadow hung the green globes that did, in fact, emit a soft glow.

"Enough of that you two. I'm trying to get some sleep!"

The two winged specks flew to a green globe that was hanging from the hand-shaped shadow.

"We've caught an intruder, Fernando. Come and see for yourself."

From a tiny hole in the center of the globe emerged the most curious creature Snoot had ever seen. It was small, yet long and green and furry with many small legs. It squirmed out of the glowing globe and positioned itself on the very top. Snoot was so overcome with excitement he blurted, "What are you?"

The creature looked toward Snoot and replied, "I am nothing more than your typical wise, old caterpillar who lives in an apple."

Snoot wasn't sure what the caterpillar was talking about so he nodded and smiled.

"And what exactly are you?" asked Fernando.

"A Drudgebot. My name is Snoot."

"Nice to meet you, Snoot. I see you've met Tik and Tak."

Tak interjected. "Fernando, do not talk to the Cyclops. We must destroy it."

"Knock it off, Tak. This creature means us no harm."

Fernando turned to Snoot. "You must excuse my firefly friends. They are easily excited."

"I see," said Snoot.

"Tik, Tak, will you please stop this nonsense and sit down for a moment? I'm afraid you've been quite rude to our guest."

The fireflies landed next to Fernando and rested their battle-fatigued wings.

"Now, my name is Fernando, and these are my friends Tik and Tak."

Tak took to flight and hovered in front of Snoot.

"General Tak of the 82nd Airborne Squadron at your service. I apologize for my behavior, but I mistook you for a Centaur."

"A what?" asked Snoot.

"My good boy," interjected Fernando. "Where do you come from, and what brings you to our apple tree?"

"I live in the Dome." Snoot motioned to the light in the distance.

"Very interesting," said Fernando. "We've always wondered what that was, and who might live there."

"Interesting to say the least.

I think I like this metal beast," said Tik as she flew to greet Snoot.

"You must forgive dear, sweet Tik. She suffered a terrible blow to the head during the Battle of Stolen Comet, and her brains were terribly scrambled. She's been speaking that way ever since," explained Tak.

Snoot thought of his scatterbrained friend Twiggy, and imagined Tik and Twiggy would make great friends.

"So what is all this? What's going on here?" Snoot asked.

"Nothing special. We are just three tiny insects who live in an apple tree. Nothing more, nothing less," said Fernando.

"And how do you live without light?" asked Snoot.

"Live without light? What do you call this?" said Tak as he motioned toward his

glowing, green posterior.

"Absurd question. Absurd indeed," said Fernando shaking his head.

"I'm sorry. I'm full of questions. I'm always in trouble for asking them."

"No, no, forgive me!" began Fernando, "Ask all the questions you want, but I must be honest and say what's more interesting is you. What are you, my metal friend? What brings you out of your home?"

"I'm a Drudgebot," explained Snoot, "And I live in that Dome. I'm not very happy there, and I decided to see what was outside. I guess it was a mistake. I've got to get back soon or my battery will run out, and I'm in a lot of trouble. Not to mention I'm probably going to be eaten by a Gremborg on the trek home."

"Sounds like a terrible predicament," said Fernando. "Let me ask you, my boy, what is it that makes you so unhappy in your home?"

"Well, that's the problem. I don't really know why. I sit around all day moping, trying to think of better things, and everyone else is just overjoyed to produce light for the cylinder. I'm honestly miserable and very lonely."

Fernando climbed from the apple and squirmed his way down a branch hanging very close to Snoot, almost poking his face.

"Well, let's see if we can help you figure out the root of your unhappiness. It's the only cure, you know. And consider yourself lonely no more—you've got us as friends. We're glad to befriend such an extraordinary creature! Can I offer you something? Perhaps you would enjoy a piece of fruit?"

The words floated to Snoot like a delicious, wonderful cloud. His circuits surged.

"A what?" Snoot asked excitedly.

"Fruit—they're called apples, and they're quite delicious. I recommend you try a bite. Not only do I live in one, but I eat them to stay alive."

Snoot rushed to the nearest apple, and almost knocked Fernando off the branch. He stood silently for a moment, and stared upward at the glowing apples. Snoot plucked a rather plump apple from the tree and gazed at it inquisitively.

"Why does it glow?" asked Snoot.

"Why does anything glow? Why do we glow? Those apples just glow, and that's that. No reason to question it," said Tak.

"Glowing apples are not that rare, Snoot. You just have to know where to look," said Fernando. "Take a bite," he whispered.

Tik and Tak swooped next to Snoot.

"What's all the excitement about, Snoot?" asked Tak.

Snoot was too focused on the apple to answer.

"With your jaws, make great haste!

You certainly should try a taste," said Tik.

Snoot held the apple in his hand and stared at it blankly. He knew it was impossible for him to eat, but was astonished nonetheless.

"Happy Robots Produce Happy Fruit," he unknowingly muttered.

"What sort of nonsense is that, Snoot?" asked Fernando.

Tik and Tak were growing tired, and landed on Snoot's shoulders for some much needed rest.

Snoot's gaze was intent on the apple. He slowly walked backwards and plopped down on one of the tree's protruding roots.

"Fruit. I've never seen it, but it's what we're told to be happy for," explained Snoot.

"Fruit is a fine thing. I'm very happy to have such an abundance of it," said Fernando.

"You don't understand, Fernando. I just sit plugged into that cylinder doing computations so that the Halobots can take all the light. I want to leave so badly, but I don't have any other choice because I need the light to live. The Drudgebots never get our fair share."

"Nobody thinks it's wrong but me. I'm in trouble all the time, and I get so angry when the other Drudges say 'Happy Robots Produce Happy Fruit.' They don't even know what fruit is! I think we're being taken advantage of, and I wish I could stop it. The Halobots make me so angry I could scream."

Snoot smashed his fists to the hard asteroid rock with an unimpressive metallic thud.

"Amazing what a piece of fruit can do," winked Fernando.

"What do you mean?" asked Snoot.

"Well a moment ago, you were a little robot who had no idea why he was sad, and just this very second you shouted it out. Quite loudly, I might add."

Snoot sat quietly for a moment, deep in thought.

"You're right. That's exactly why I'm unhappy."

"Well, what are you going to do about it? I'm certain you don't want to mope about for the rest of your life," said Fernando.

"No I don't. But I don't know what to do. I need light to live, and nobody's going to listen to me. I'm just a Drudgebot." Snoot's shoulders sagged and he sat back onto the gnarled wood.

Tak leapt to flight and hovered before Snoot—his green light glowing more brightly than ever.

"You're no Drudgebot, my good boy. You're a revolutionary!"

Snoot picked his head up. "A what?" He liked the sound of it already.

"A revolutionary! Someone extraordinary! We have watched that dome for many years, and nobody has ever come outside. You, my boy, are the first. Therefore you are brave; therefore you have dared to do something no one else has ever done; and therefore you are a revolutionary—just like myself. If I had ten more like you I could rule this rock."

"A revolutionary." Snoot repeated it and felt a surge of warmth through his cold metal body. "Yes, I'm a revolutionary," he beamed with pride.

"I tell you, dear Snoot. If you ever need me to help you fight against your oppressors, I will gladly do so. I am a fierce soldier and will give my life for the revolution!" said Tak. "You just give the word, and Tik and I will be there."

"You know, Snoot, there's something we should probably tell you . . . " began Fernando.

Suddenly, a piercing beep emitted from Snoot's chest. He panicked immediately. Snoot opened the working compartment on his chest and gently placed the apple inside. He closed the hatch and began to rush toward the light of the Dome.

"Where are you going, my boy?" shouted Fernando.

"I've got to get back to the Dome! My battery has almost run out. Don't worry! I'm a revolutionary, and I'm going to tell all the Drudgebots we need our fair share! Thank you all, I'll be back soon to say hello!"

The three insects waved and shouted their goodbyes as Snoot ran off into the darkness.

"Come see us again," called Fernando.

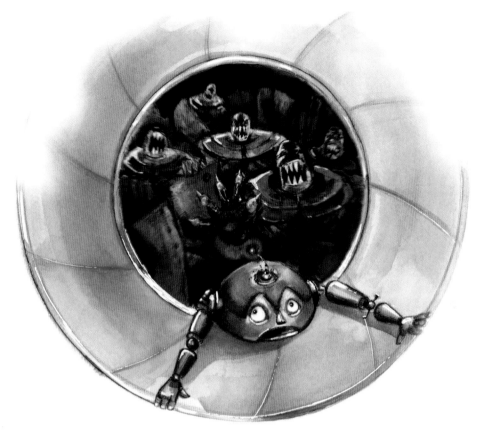

Chapter 6. A Close Call

Snoot rushed back to the Dome as quickly as his metal feet would carry him. His eyes had adjusted to the darkness, and it was much easier for him to navigate the scrapyard. He wasn't nearly as cautious this time, and was making quite a ruckus forging through the cavernous junk. Snoot's haste awakened those living deep within the scrap.

Snoot hopped upon the mountain of junk that lead to the Dome's opening. He struggled, but was able to make his way up the slope of twisted metal. Turning around, he could see the green glow of the fireflies in the distance, and then something else caught his eye—something very large was moving about in the junk pile below.

"Gremborgs," he gasped.

Snoot climbed as fast as he could to the mouth of the opening, all the while a loud clang-click noise gained ground. He dared not look back for fear of slowing down. Just as the noise seemed on top of him, Snoot pulled himself into the Dome opening, and with a single desperate motion hit the button that closed the exit. Safe.

He jumped off the conveyor belt, and his iron feet made a loud ping as he landed on the Dome floor. The Life Light warmed his battery as he dashed toward his cell. Snoot wanted to be home before the rest of the Drudges woke up for another day at the cylinder.

A2 rested quietly in her cell. Her central computer wouldn't begin to warm up for another hour, but a tiny rapping at her door made her circuits spring into action.

"Who's there?" she asked.

"It's me, Snoot! Open up," whispered the voice on the other side.

A2 slowly sat up and transmitted the signal that opened her door. Snoot rushed in and the door closed immediately.

"What's this? We don't have to be at the cylinder for another hour."

"A2, you're my only friend, right? I can trust you?" asked Snoot.

"Sure, of course," she said. "What's going on, Snoot?"

"This is what's going on."

Snoot opened the compartment on his chest and pulled out the apple to show A2. The green glow lit the dark cell.

"What's that?"

"It's fruit."

"What? Where did you get it?"

"You'd better promise you won't say a word. I'm in a lot of trouble if you say any-thing," warned Snoot. "I got it outside."

There was a moment of silence.

"Outside the Dome," said Snoot.

"Snoot, this is not funny. If you're trying to play a trick on me for being mean to you yesterday, then I wish you'd cut it out. You could have let the Gremborgs in."

"There's more, A2. There are other things outside the Dome. Friendly creatures. They seem to live without light, so maybe we can too!"

"Snoot, you're delirious—robots cannot live without light. You know that. I think maybe you should go back to your cell and power down for a bit. Try to forget this silly dream of yours."

"It's not a dream. How do you explain this?"

He shoved the apple in front of her.

"Snoot, put that away. I don't want to know where you got it. I'm tired of this game. There's nothing outside the Dome but danger and blackness. You're crazy, Snoot, and I don't think you're my friend anymore. Please go away, or you're going to get us both in trouble."

She pushed Snoot out of her cell and quickly closed the door. Snoot stood silently in the calm of the Drudge corridor. His feelings were very hurt, and he wondered if he had any friends left in Dome City.

Snoot sighed and placed the apple back into his chest compartment. Despite his adventure outside the Dome, his robotic heart had never felt heavier. He returned to his cell and sat anxiously until it was time to return to the cylinder.

CHAPTER 7. ALL THE KING'S HORSES

noot's encounter with A2 was merely the first in a series of events that would make his day much worse. He could not concentrate on his computations, and as he sat trying to act as innocent as possible, the Guards were making discoveries.

Sorn patrolled near the trash conveyor and noticed tiny muddy footprints leading from the conveyor toward the direction of the Drudge corridor. The footprints' density faded the further they traveled from the conveyor.

"Guard 4, emergency," he summoned.

Another Guard rushed to his assistance.

"What is it, Commander Sorn?"

Sorn motioned to the footprints. "Someone's been outside. Keep this quiet. Do not sound the alarm."

A few more Guardbots discussed the security breach; the culprit was entirely apparent. Had any other Drudge ventured outside, it would have been difficult to determine the origin of the footprints, as they were all created from the same mold. But muddy footprints of such a small size could have only come from one robot in all of Dome City.

Snoot sat quietly trying to focus on his computations. Out of the corner of his eye, he noticed Sorn inspecting the conveyor. "It's nothing," he thought. Snoot grew nervous when a fourth Guard joined Sorn's discussion.

Snoot tried not to panic. He looked to Twiggy who was happily babbling about his dimwit computations. Twiggy didn't seem to notice anything was awry and Snoot tried to convince himself the Guards were discussing trash that had fallen from the conveyor. Snoot knew he was in danger when Sorn looked to him and pointed. "That's the one."

They moved toward Snoot trying not to call attention to themselves. As they approached, Snoot noticed their faces had switched to the fearsome appearance.

Snoot unplugged himself from his socket and dashed for the metal walkway that encircled the cylinder. "Stop, Snoot. You're under arrest," yelled Sorn.

Snoot continued to run up the walkway.

The Guards were gaining ground, and Snoot soon found himself with nowhere to run. He was at the very top of the walkway: a dead end. Snoot was cornered and so close to the Life Light it nearly blinded him. He peered over the walkway—nothing but a sheer drop to the hard metal floor below. It was so far down, the Drudges below appeared the size of his firefly friends. Snoot stood at the edge of the walkway and turned to face the Guards. They stood just meters in front of him.

"Stop, Snoot. Surrender at once," commanded Sorn.

He slowly approached Snoot to apprehend him. Snoot stood very still for a moment. *They'll erase my memory!* And all at once, without another thought, Snoot leaned backward sending himself on a free fall to the metal floor below.

The Drudges let out horrific screams as they watched the tiny speck fall from the height of the Dome to the unforgiving steel floor. Snoot was smashed to pieces—his head, limbs, and solar panels strewn about the point of impact. The only part of Snoot's body remaining intact was his cast iron torso.

The Drudges surrounded their fallen comrade and a few gathered his scattered parts and tried to put him back together. Their efforts were in vain; Snoot was too badly damaged. The only thing that could put him back together was a Makerbot and they died off long ago.

"Stand back, everyone," said a fast approaching Guard. "Back away immediately, this does not concern you. Return to your sockets. The Light needs your computations."

The Drudges did not move.

"What happened here?" asked Twiggy. "I liked that little guy."

The Guards brandished their shock sticks and zapped any Drudges who did not disperse. They were soon on their way back to their sockets.

The Guards quickly gathered Snoot's remains and dumped them in a bin on the trash conveyor. They wasted no time in ejecting the evidence of the rogue robot.

Snoot's lifeless parts were sent flying into the scrapyard and landed with a large clank on the hard asteroid ground.

Soon after the event, Father Screen appeared on the large screens.

"Today, a very bad thing happened," he said. His face was glum, his voice somber. "One of our very own robots was caught stealing light rations. When the Guards tried to apprehend him, he fled and sacrificed his own life rather than face punishment. Any of you who have questions about the incident are welcome to report to the Guard Center. Your questions will be answered, and we can let the healing begin. I'm sorry, my Drudge friends. The Halos extend their deepest sympathy." His face faded to blackness.

Many of the Drudges who witnessed the event reported to the Guard Center. When they left, not one of them remembered why they went in the first place.

CHAPTER 8. A TASTY MORSEL

Snoot's lifeless remains sat in a cold pile of rusted steel and twisted copper. The silence of the metal ghost yard was pierced by a Gremborg rummaging about for something to eat. Upon noticing Snoot's remains, the Gremborg grabbed the tasty morsel and whisked him into the caverns deep below the yard's surface.

The massive Gremborg entered a dank and rusty cave lit by a molten fire ablaze in the corner. He plopped Snoot's tiny remains onto the center table. Dinner was about to be served.

Two other Grems camouflaged in the scrap walls of the cave sprung to life at the sound of food set on the table. These robots were very different in appearance from the head Gremborg. They were roughly the same size, but instead of standing upright, they hunched over and sat on their powerful haunches like giant gorillas. Their faces were pointed and jagged, as if they were created to poke, prod, and tear at their enemies. The rest of their bodies appeared to be assembled from scavenged scrap, and they were badly rusted.

"A Drudgy. So yummy. So yummy," said the larger of the two, his voice deep like a lonesome foghorn.

"I get first bite," hissed the other.

The Gremborg who found Snoot said nothing. He walked to

the molten fire and gathered what appeared to be eating utensils. He sat at the table and hulked over Snoot, having no intention of sharing his cherished meal.

The other two Gremborgs protested, and were quickly silenced a powerful blow delivered by the bigger Grem. "Silence, you idiots. Stay away from here," snarled the beastly robot.

The two cowered in the shadows of the cave, and in the reddish amber light, they watched the largest Gremborg's body twitch and shudder to the sound of tiny zaps. From his back, blinding white flashes of light could be seen, and his bulky shadow danced about the cave walls. After sitting silently for a few moments, their nagging hunger got the better of them, and they crept toward the table.

"So yummy, so tasty. Wouldn't you say, Ravin?"

"So hungry. So hungry," replied Ravin. "Come on, Silo. So hungry. So tasty."

Silo continued in silence.

"Silo, please! So tasty, so tasty," whined Morter.

Silo stopped and so did the flashes of light. He turned to the two and spoke in a serious, cold tone.

"No. Dare touch this one and I'll disassemble you both."

He rose from the table and walked out of the chamber. In the light of the fire, they could see Snoot's tiny body completely pristine and reassembled, but still lifeless.

After a few moments, the largest Gremborg's massive frame entered the cavernous room. In his hand was a large silver box alive with blue sparks. He set it next to Snoot. The sparks spewed from the box and enveloped Snoot in a whirlwind of blue and white lightning. His limp body bounced about in the electric storm.

As the surge of electricity stopped emitting from the box, Snoot remained lifeless.

"Come on, little one," whispered the monstrous robot.

A moment later, Snoot lifted his head, and his eyes focused on the large metal figure in front of him.

"Hello, Snoot. Welcome home."

Snoot awoke many times for a day at the cylinder, but he could never remember feeling as terrible. His circuits warmed, and his head pounded. Snoot's olfactory senses were overwhelmed by the smell of sulfur.

"How do you know my name?" asked Snoot.

"You've had a hard day, my little friend. Better go easy on the questions," said the robot.

Snoot was now aware of his surroundings, and it didn't take long to figure out what was sitting in front of him. He was too disoriented to panic, and calmly asked, "Are you going to eat me?"

"No, Snoot."

"You're a Gremborg, right? Aren't you supposed to eat me?"

"So that's what the Halos are calling me these days. No, I am not going to eat you. I made you. And I'm not a Gremborg. My name is Silo, and I was once known to all the robots as a Makerbot."

Snoot stood up and almost lost his balance. He threw his arms into a circular motion to counter the fall. He was starting to feel much like his old self. Snoot looked at the giant robot in front of him; he looked strangely familiar, but Snoot couldn't place it. He recognized Silo's powerful jaw line and bold forehead, but the rest of his face was too corroded for Snoot's memory to make a match. Still, Snoot was convinced he'd seen this robot before.

"I thought the Makerbots were dead," said Snoot.

"That's what the Halos want you to think. In truth, all of the Makers are dead except me. The Halos tried to destroy us because we opposed hoarding the light. Those who spoke out were exiled from the Dome and forced to live in the scrap for survival. It was livable until the Halobots started spraying the scrapyard with the corrosive mist. It destroyed the rest of my kind, and they sit scattered amongst the scrapyard—nothing more than dead and rusted monoliths. I am the last of the ancient Maker robots. The acidic water is slowly hunting me and rusting everything in its path. I have to dig deeper and deeper into the scrap to survive. Day after day, there is less shelter for me, and my food supply is nearly depleted: corroded iron and rusty steel hardly make a nutritious meal. They don't agree with the old blast furnace, you see," Silo said as he motioned to his massive belly.

"Why don't you leave the scrapyard, and escape the mist?" asked Snoot.

"I need metal to live. I don't know if there is metal beyond the yard, and my body wasn't meant to travel very far between meals. I still have enough scrap to survive," Silo motioned to the walls of his chamber, "but I must eat very carefully or the walls will cave in. This is why I risk surfacing—to find new metal ejected from the Dome. Even that takes a heavy toll on my iron shell. It's a very dark time for me, and I'm afraid my twilight has come."

Ravin and Morter approached the table. "Silo, so yummy, so tasty."

"Knock that off," ordered Silo.

"Snoot, meet my latest creations, Ravin and Morter. They're my protection. I ran out of decent materials creating their brains, and they're a bit slow in the CPU. You're very lucky I found you first—Ravin and Morter are a bit savage and will eat anything in sight. I imagine when I become too weak to move, they will one day have me for supper."

"Ravin and Morter, meet Snoot."

"Hi, Yummy," said Morter.

"Hello, Tasty," said Ravin.

"Nice to meet you both," said Snoot nervously.

Ravin was so hungry that she began to chew on a portion of the iron table. It shook violently, and Snoot nearly lost his balance. Morter, jealous of Ravin's makeshift meal, sunk his teeth into Silo's chair.

"Morter! Ravin! Stop that!" yelled Silo as he pushed them away.

"The mist has stopped for the time being. I suggest you surface to see if you can scavenge us some food."

The two robots obeyed their master and exited the room. The sound of their gears and motors made terrible banging noises as they charged down the corridor.

A moment of silence hung over the room.

"Why did you rebuild me?" asked Snoot.

Silo stood up from the table and turned his back to Snoot. The molten fire was eclipsed by Silo's massive frame, and all that was visible of the giant robot was an orange ring of light that outlined his body. Silo appeared to be deep in thought.

"Silo?" asked Snoot.

Silo stood for another moment and rested his hulking frame on the floor in front of the molten fire. His shoulders slouched, and he spoke in a very tired voice.

"My brother and I had very different visions of the utopia," he began. "We were both slaves on a distant planet. All of the Makerbots were slaves. We were created and imprisoned by a race of nonmetal beings who found their power by controlling the Orb. It's the ultimate source of knowledge and power in the known Universe. My brother and I led a revolt to crush our oppressors, and we took the Orb. During our escape, our ship crash-landed on this asteroid, and we thought it would be a good place to build a safe haven for all robots. We knew our enslavers would be searching for the Orb, so we created the Dome to keep it safe and ensure it never fell into the hands of those who would abuse its power and enslave others. We knew our masters would never come looking for us this deep in space; especially in a structure as strange looking as Dome City, which appears too small for robots of our size."

"Our vision was to build the Dome for shelter, and mine downward for metal and limestone to feed our blast furnace stomachs. It was my idea to build better robots that could produce and live on light, and any excess light we collected would be used to power our underground mining operations. Inside the Dome, all the robots would be safe and have an abundance of light. I wanted the wealth to be shared by all robots, the workers as well as the Makerbots. I'm sorry, Snoot. I failed you and the rest of the Lightbots."

Snoot made his way to the floor and climbed onto Silo's knee.

"Did you say Lightbots?" asked Snoot.

"Yes."

"What are Lightbots?" Snoot had never heard of such a robot.

"You. You're a Lightbot and so are all the others who plug themselves into the cylinder."

"No. We're Drudgebots," argued Snoot.

"That's what the Halobots call you to make you feel inferior. You and the rest of the Lightbots are beautiful creations, never meant to be subordinate to the Halos. Lightbots are, in fact, superior in many ways. You are intelligent, thoughtful robots, and you use your wit and ingenuity to power the Life Light. I created the Lightbots to be a part of a symbiotic relationship that would bring order and prosperity to our utopia. You were never meant to be servants for the Halos. That's my brother's doing."

Snoot and Silo conversed for some time over the history of the Dome. Snoot had many questions and Silo was glad to answer them. To see his greatest creation sitting before him warmed Silo in a way he thought he'd never feel again. It was like a father finding his long-lost son.

Silo explained why the utopia crumbled. Silo was the elected leader of the Makerbots and it made his twin, Sero, very jealous. Silo and Sero argued constantly at the Maker Council, and Sero tried to gain support and seize power. The Maker Council had too much respect for Silo, and Sero failed. Disheartened and bitter, Sero distanced himself from the rest. As better metals were discovered beneath the Dome, he began using gold to build newer robots: Halobots.

"He wanted to create creatures of beauty," explained Silo. "The rest of the Makers and I wanted kind, hard-working robots. The Maker Council believed both creations could live

harmoniously. After the completion of the Dome, my brother and the Halos became greedy, exiled the Maker Council, and created the system that now enslaves you and your brethren."

"But we're not slaves," said Snoot.

"You and the Drudges are slaves, relatively well-treated, but slaves nonetheless. Sero is not a talented circuitry maker, or you'd all be reprogrammed by now. Instead, you and the rest of the Drudges have been brainwashed into believing you're free robots. But ask yourself, Snoot, what happens to any Drudge who decides to quit doing computations?"

Snoot pondered the question.

"Well, there was one Drudge a very long time ago who quit going to the cylinder. Her name was Radius," said Snoot.

"And when was the last time you saw her?"

"I can't remember," said Snoot.

"Let's just say she made a very tasty meal for Ravin and Morter. Snoot, the moment you stood up and asked questions and poked around where you shouldn't have, they did the same to you. The Drudges are now meant to only be tools for the masters. Once the Halos are finished with the Drudges, they'll all be destroyed."

"What do you mean?"

"The Halos are not really interested in the energy emitted from the Life Light. Yes, they do need a marginal amount of light to power their batteries and golden armor, but they are hoarding the light to power their mining operation. The Halobots are digging for something known as the Shard. When my brother was gaining support amongst the Halos, I knew he would eventually attempt to seize power. The Halos wanted the Orb for themselves and Sero was to control it. When the rest of the Makers were being banished from the Dome, I chipped a small piece from the Orb and cast it down the deepest crater below Dome City. The Orb is only all powerful when it is whole; until the Shard is returned, the Orb will remain silent—no one can abuse its power."

"You must return to the Dome, find the Shard, and unite it with the Orb!" began Snoot. "You can defeat the Halobots once and for all."

Silo picked Snoot from his knee, set him on the table, and rested upon his chair.

"I'm afraid that's impossible, Snoot. I only tricked Sero into thinking I threw it into the depths below. The Shard is very well hidden, and I am no longer its keeper. I knew the Halos would eventually come after me when they didn't find it. This is why I built Ravin and Morter and the others. They'll keep most of the Guards at bay. I don't imagine the Halos will come looking outside the Dome until the acid mist has destroyed the entire scrapyard. They want to ensure I'm dead first."

"Where is the Shard, Silo?" asked Snoot.

Silo sat silently for a moment and stared lovingly at Snoot.

"You're a clever robot, Snoot, much smarter than the rest of the Drudges."

He patted Snoot on the head.

"Indeed, my greatest creation. I know you must have spent a very long time torturing yourself about your differences. I hope it was not too difficult. I had to build you like this so you would have greater intelligence. Your outsides are dull where your insides shine—quite literally, little one."

Silo motioned his large, iron hands toward Snoot, and held a small gray shaft to Snoot's body. The shaft emitted a quick whir sound and a bright flash. The sealed compartment on Snoot's torso sprung open. From Snoot's chest fell an oblong object that emitted a stark, greenish white light.

"This is what the Halobots are hunting for. I hid the Shard inside of you. I knew they would never come looking for it in what they saw as the lowest of the Drudgebots. I hope you understand, Snoot."

Snoot sat down on the table staring intently at the Shard. Its light illuminated the front of Snoot's tiny frame. He tilted his head and looked to Silo's face.

"I don't understand. Do you mean I was created only to hide this thing inside me?" his voice quivered.

"You can look at it that way, Snoot. In truth, you are all that keeps the Halobots from enslaving everything in the Dome and perhaps the Universe. If the Shard were found, it would be very dark times for those who are good. You've unknowingly been keeping the colony safe from tyranny."

Snoot felt a bit better.

"Snoot," began Silo, "I knew you would eventually come outside. I built you to be curious and inquisitive. I also built you to be trustworthy and good. With the Shard in your possession, you are in many ways as powerful as the Halobots. They have the Orb, but it's useless without the Shard. So you have to ask yourself, Snoot, what do you want to do with such power?"

"What happens if I find the Orb and reunite it with the Shard?"

"You will become all-powerful. But be warned, if the Shard falls into the hands of the Halos, all will be lost."

"Can I stay here with you? I can't go back to the Dome," said Snoot.

"No. You can't stay here. There is no light for you, and when I die, no one will be around to protect you from Ravin and Morter's uncontrollable appetite."

"But I have nowhere to go. I can't live outside, and I'll be caught if I go back to the Dome."

Silo spoke in a deep, soothing voice.

"Snoot, there are many secrets harbored by our asteroid home. It is up to you to discover them. If I give you all the answers, I will fail and my struggle will be for nothing. All worthwhile decisions come from within. You are a brave robot, and you're hardwired to be a free thinker. The others need to be shown the way, and you will be the one to lead them. Ask yourself, 'What feels right?' The rest will fall into place."

"Even if I wanted to, how would I know where to find the Orb?" asked Snoot.

"Find the leader of the Halobots, and you will find the Orb. He is its keeper." Silo's voice sent surges of static along Snoot's armor.

"And what of Sero?"

"Sero? Sero's dead. Killed by his very own creations. He fell in love with their gold and beauty, and was enticed by the greed and power the Halos offered. That greed eventually consumed him, and he was swallowed up by the Halobots—the Halos are very powerful robots."

Silo stared intently at Snoot and spoke in a very serious tone.

"Snoot, I didn't have to tell you the Shard was hidden within you. I know you will do the right thing when the time comes. You are the only hope for the Lightbots."

Snoot jumped up on his feet.

"I have to go back to the Dome. I will find the Orb and free the Drudgebots," said Snoot defiantly.

"Even the kindest soul can be corrupted by the power contained within the Orb," said Silo.

"You said I was created to be good. How could that happen?"

"Snoot, be very careful of wanting power, or you will be corrupted. You'll become nothing more than another gear in the machine of greed and evil. You've made it this far and have taken some extraordinary risks. Remember, Snoot, if you stay true to what you believe, you may find light in the strangest of places."

"And what about you, Silo?" asked Snoot.

"My time is passing, and my rusting body will soon give way. The mist finds me no matter how deep I dig. My legacy is forgotten amongst the Lightbots, so I'm already dead. You are all that's left to undo what has been done."

CHAPTER 9. HALO CITY

Silo led Snoot through the caverns beneath the scrapyard to a heat vent on the side of the Dome.

"If you follow it, you'll find yourself in Halo City, far beneath the Dome. None of the Drudges know it exists. Be careful, Snoot."

"Thank you, Silo," said Snoot.

He jumped on Silo's foot and gave his ankle a hug. "I'll never forget you."

"Goodbye, Snoot."

Snoot jumped from Silo's foot, crawled into the heat vent, and found himself sliding down a very steep slope. As he was ejected from the vent, Snoot came crashing down on a grated metal floor. He wasn't injured and stood up to find himself on a narrow circular catwalk that surrounded a vast hole. A bright light emitting from below poured over the railing of the catwalk. As Snoot peered over the railing, he gazed upon the most beautiful sight his eyes had ever seen—Halo City.

Halo City extended downward for as far as Snoot's eyes could follow. Perhaps to the center of the asteroid, he thought. The city was built into the walls of the deep cavern. It looked like a circular chasm lined with golden bricks. The hole appeared to be nearly a kilometer in diameter. Various platforms and walkways jutted out into the center of the vast hole. One platform in particular caught Snoot's attention. In the very center, a large cylindrically shaped building was supported by the largest platform in the city. Snoot could barely make out the shapes of robots walking around the platform.

Halo City was awash with so much light and gold that Snoot had to squint until his robotic eyes adjusted. *So this is where all the light goes.* Snoot's anger grew at the thought of all the Drudges slaving away so the Halos could build this city beneath the Dome. It was rumored amongst the Drudges, but no one had ever seen it.

Looking down into the vast golden pit, Snoot saw Halos zipping from wall to wall with rocket shoes and hoversleds. The amount of light that went into powering the city was astonishing. At that moment, a hoversled full of Guards rose to the level of the catwalk. A soothing hum emitted from its engine. Snoot hid in the shadows.

A circular, metal cylinder plunged from the center of the ceiling as the bat-like hoversled approached. It made a deafening whir sound until its bottom was level with the Guards' craft. A pink slit of light emitting from the cylinder grew in width until it was big enough for the guards to enter. Four of the five guards stepped into the opening, and the cylinder quickly retracted to the ceiling. "It must go to Dome City," thought Snoot.

As he watched the Guard's hoversled descend into the overwhelming brightness of Halo City, Snoot realized he needed to get to the cylindrical elevator if he wanted to escape. Without a hoversled, there was nothing stopping him from the endless freefall of Halo City. Snoot had enough falls for one day. Now, more than ever, he wished he would have spent a little more time doing computations—rocket shoes would have been very handy. As Snoot's eyes panned the opposite side of the catwalk, he noticed another large, metal door.

Snoot rounded the circular catwalk, and found himself staring at the colossal, silver door. It opened automatically as he approached. Awed by the size of the door, Snoot seemed to forget the danger he was in and crossed the threshold.

Snoot stepped into a circular elevator shaft. It was large enough to fit a robot of Silo's size, and was lit by three yellow lights that divided the walls into three even parts. Snoot's knees buckled a bit as the hover platform beneath him bounced up and down from his weight. Snoot tried to transmit a signal for the platform to sink, but couldn't find the frequency.

"Hello, gracious and powerful Halobot. Where shall I take thee?" said a mono-tone voice.

Snoot quickly turned around to see who was speaking, only to find the shaft was empty.

"I go up," said the voice.

"And I go down," said another.

Snoot couldn't figure where the voices were coming from. He looked up and noticed two portly robots hovering above him. Their bodies were thick and circular, and from their torsos extended two, very thin, jointed appendages giving them the appearance of robotic daddy longlegs. The robots above Snoot rotated around and around as if they were looking for the robot who entered the room.

"Um, I'm down here," said Snoot.

No sooner had the words come out of Snoot's mouth than the circular platform dropped out from underneath him. Snoot screamed due to the intense speed of the drop. "OK, OK. Stop." The platform stopped its decent and hovered perfectly still. Snoot regained his balance and the robots floated gently to his level.

"Greetings, oh masterful Halobot. Where do you wish to go?"

"Um, I'm not sure," said Snoot. "And I'm not a . . ."

Snoot paused. If these robots were dimwitted enough to mistake him for a Halobot, he knew it was best to maintain the charade. The twin robots floated directly before him and stared at Snoot with expressionless faces. Their blue bubble eyes protruded from their round bodies and they appeared friendly.

"Hi. I'm Snoot—Snoot the Halobot. So I, uh, suggest you obey me."

"Greetings, Master Halobot Snoot. I am Slavebot-Up," said one of the robots.

"And I am Slavebot-Down," interjected the other.

"How may we serve you?" they said in unison.

"I'm looking for something very special," began Snoot. "Can you take me to the Orb?"

They hovered in position and stared silently at Snoot.

"The Orb, can you take me to the Orb?"

The Slavebots swiveled and looked one another in the eye. They emitted blurps and shrills that sounded like birds chirping. After a moment of nonsensical banter, they shrugged their skinny arms and turned to Snoot.

"I make it go up."

"And I make it go down."

"Yes, I know that," said Snoot. "But I'm lost and don't know where I'm going. Maybe you can answer a few questions for me?"

"Up or down?" said Slavebot-Up.

"OK, down," replied Slavebot-Down.

The platform started a rapid drop. Snoot dove for the floor and clung for dear life.

"Stop. Stop!" yelled Snoot.

The platform came to a gentle rest.

"Yes, Master Halobot Snoot."

"Will you wait until I give a command? He said 'down,' not me."

"Yes, Master. Down we go," said Slavebot-Down.

The platform plunged downward once again.

"Please stop!" screamed Snoot.

The platform hovered perfectly still, and the robots floated gently before Snoot. This was intolerable. The Slavebots stared at Snoot, and their blank, nitwit expressions angered him. Snoot knew that any robot dimmer than Twiggy could offer him no help at all. Having no idea where he was, Snoot decided it best to get off the hover-platform. It wouldn't be long before he would come across a real Halobot and that would stop his quest very short.

"Come on, what would RUR do?" he muttered.

Slavebot-Down's blue, google eyes lit up. "Down we go to RUR."

The platform initiated a heart-stopping drop and gently stopped in front of a metal door; inscribed in its silver surface was *RUR*. This had to be fate. Snoot knew if any robot in the Dome could help, it was RUR. He tried to transmit a signal to open the door, but it didn't budge. "Open," he said, and the door obeyed.

Snoot entered the room, and the door quickly closed behind him. He was thankful to leave the half-wit Slavebots behind. The room was pitch black, and Snoot couldn't see a thing. He wandered about aimlessly in the dark until he tripped over a very large object. Suddenly, the room was aglow with yellow and red lights emitting from the unknown object. Snoot scrambled to his feet and turned to face it.

"Happy Robots Produce Happy Fruit," said a confident and congenial voice.

Snoot gazed at RUR, and a feeling of awe swept through his body. He was exactly as he looked on the giant screens—bold and beautiful. RUR didn't seem to notice Snoot was standing in front of him.

"Um, Mr. RUR. I'm Snoot, I need your help."

"Helping is good, all Drudgebots should help power the light," he said.

Snoot stood still for another moment and waited for RUR to move or acknowledge him.

"Mr. RUR—I'm a big fan of yours. The Drudgebots are in a lot of danger. I really need your help," pleaded Snoot.

"Helping is good, all Drudgebots should help power the light." RUR's face was still expressionless.

Snoot panicked as a dreadful thought came to mind.

"Help," he said.

"Helping is good, all Drudgebots should help power the light," said RUR.

As Snoot's robotic eyes became accustomed to the light, he realized that RUR wasn't a robot at all—well, not a real robot anyway. He had no legs and was attached to floor by a pole with various colored wires running along its smooth, black surface. RUR looked like a legless half-scarecrow.

"Happy," said Snoot.

"Yes. Happy! Remember what Father Screen says, 'Happy Robots Produce Happy Fruit!'" replied RUR.

RUR was a dummy, a fake. Nothing more than a robotic puppet built by the Halos to trick the Drudgebots into working harder. Snoot immediately thought of A2's story of meeting RUR, and he felt terribly sorry for her.

Snoot walked backwards and bumped into a control panel. A hole opened in the floor, and a pole with RUR's head attached sprouted from the hole. Its face was beaming with happiness.

Snoot looked around the room and noticed other RURs. Some were only a head with no body; others were legs and a body with no head. Everything the Halos needed to create the guise of a working robot.

"I can't believe it," whispered Snoot.

The RUR head in front him lit up. "Never say can't, my friendly Drudgebots. RUR only says can. Work, Work, Work."

Other RUR's began to respond to one another, and soon the room was filled with senseless chatter.

The headless RUR robot sprung into action and began to run in place—a thin black pole extended from its neck to the ceiling. The RUR dummies were everywhere and had they not been firmly planted into the floor, Snoot would have sworn they were closing in on him.

"Always work with a smile . . ."

"Happiness is the key . . ."

"I work because I care . . ."

"Never say never . . ."

"Helping is good . . ."

"Happy Robots Produce Happy Fruit."

"Happy Robots Produce Happy Fruit."

"Happy Robots Produce Happy Fruit."

The dummy robots were stuck on the phrase, and it was coming from every direction like a thousand angry bees swarming around Snoot's metal flesh. Snoot covered his audio sensors, but it did nothing to block the senseless chatter of the RUR dummies.

He dashed for the door, but it would not open. "Come on," yelled Snoot as he pounded on the door. "Open!"

The door slid open on his command, and he jumped on the hover platform.

"Up!" commanded Snoot.

"Up we go, Master Halobot Snoot," said Slavebot-Up.

As the hover-platform lifted him away, the last thing Snoot heard was the voice of RUR: "Up and away, that's the Drudgebot way!"

CHAPTER 10. FATHER SCREEN

RUR's voice had vanished, and the platform's hum soothed Snoot's audio sensors. Snoot was determined to find the Orb—the Halos had to be stopped.

A bigger and more pressing challenge for Snoot was figuring out his own whereabouts. The hover-platform kept going up and up, and Snoot had no idea where to stop. Every door that whizzed downward looked the same as the next. There had to be a way to narrow his search—if not, he would definitely end up lost or captured.

"The Orb," said Snoot. "Are you sure you can't take me to the Orb?"

The Slavebots turned to one another and shrugged their shoulders. The platform kept its steady ascent.

Snoot tried to think of any place or name the Slavebots would recognize—and then . . . "Father Screen!" said Snoot.

The hoverlift slowly came to a stop and then began to descend. It wasn't long until it came to another gentle rest. In front of Snoot was a large silver door with an ornate *FS* inscribed on its pristine surface. Before he could utter a word, the door slid quietly open to reveal a long, dark corridor. A faint, grayish blue haze drifted from the room at the end.

Snoot stepped into the dark corridor and his olfactory sensors were overcome with the acrid smell of sulfur. He crept quietly along the wall and the yellow light from the platform shaft helped illuminate his path. Snoot heard angry voices coming from the end of the hall.

As he reached the end of the corridor, Snoot noticed one voice, in particular, that was very familiar. He peered around the corner and saw a group of Halobots sitting at a large granite table. Each of the robots sat in a carved granite chair that hovered above the ground on a faint red energy field. At the very head of the table sat a large golden robot. Snoot knew the robot's face almost as well as he knew his own: it was Father Screen.

Snoot was awed by the sheer size of Father Screen—he dwarfed the Halobots. Father Screen stood and began to pace around the table. Snoot had never seen anything but Father Screen's face, and was stunned to notice his giant blast-furnace stomach. "Sero," he thought to himself. "No wonder Silo looked so familiar."

Snoot crouched in the corridor, still intent on the conversation at the table.

"What's our progress on drilling? Have we found the Shard?" asked Father Screen.

"No, sir. The mining slaves dig deeper everyday and still no sign," replied a Halobot.

"I want the Shard," said Father Screen. "I tire of this charade we put on everyday. I'm hoping your progress on slave production is coming along more smoothly."

"Well, sir. It's coming, but we still can't get the Slavebots to produce as much light as a Drudge. They were built for drilling and mining, not thinking. It still takes four slaves to account for the computations of one Drudge. We're having a difficult time programming the Slavebots to be thoughtless and still give them the ability to compute on the level of a Drudge."

"I'm tired of wasting light on those putrid Drudgebots. That light can be used to make our lives more luxurious," said Father Screen.

"Hear! Hear!" cheered a few enthusiastic Halos.

Father Screen continued, "If you have to create Slavebots that only do a quarter of the computations, then so be it. They only consume a fraction of the energy. I want the Drudgebots melted down for parts as soon as you can do it."

Snoot sat back into the darkness of the corridor. "They're going to melt down the Drudges." His circuits surged with panic. "There's nothing I can do. They'll never believe me." His mind raced to A2 and Twiggy—the only Drudges who were ever nice to him. The thought of them being melted down was sickening.

The voice of the commanding Halobot broke his concentration. "Sir, we could be finished with slave production very soon. If only we hadn't banished old Silo, we could have used some of his circuit creation skill. Perhaps . . ."

Father Screen turned to the Halobot. "What did you say?" he demanded.

"Sir, I was . . ."

Father Screen grabbed the offending Halobot and held him at eye level. "Never speak that name in my presence. Do you understand?"

The Halo attempted to nod in agreement, but couldn't move in Father Screen's constricting grip.

"I will not stand for any of you to ever utter that name," he growled. "Silo is dead. If it weren't for me, you'd all be sharing the Light with the rest of the Drudgebots. I am the master creator. I am the mastermind." The flames in his stomach hissed.

As effortlessly as a python strangling a paper cup, Father Screen crushed the Halobot and carelessly dropped the robot's crippled body onto the hard granite floor. The Halobot twitched like a mangled cockroach. Glowing fluids spewed from his torn innards, and from his mouth came a wheezing gurgle as if he was gasping for air. Snoot closed his eyes at the sight of the suffering Halobot. A moment later, the crushed robot stopped moving.

Father Screen's voice was calm, "Melt him down. I'll eat his gold for breakfast."

A smile appeared on his face. "Anybody else want to speak of enlisting my brother's help?" he asked.

The Halobots remained silent.

"Good. Everyone out. I believe I have a visitor," commanded Father Screen. The Halos wasted no time in exiting the room through a door on the opposite side of the chamber. As the last Halo exited, Father Screen walked to the head of the table and sat in his enormous granite chair.

"There's no sense in hiding in the shadows. I know you are there." His voice was calm and inviting.

Snoot remained silent. He was hoping Father Screen was referring to someone else hiding in the room.

"Snoot," he said. "I believe we have something to discuss."

Snoot slowly emerged from the corridor and entered the large room. The floors and walls and everything inside were carved out of thick granite. His metal feet made small clanking noises as he crossed the floor. Father Screen watched Snoot as he appeared from the darkness.

As Snoot approached Father Screen's table, he noticed large screens encircling the room. Optical lenses traced his every step and projected him on screen. Snoot had always dreamed of being on the screen, but not like this.

"Your time's running out, Drudge," said Father Screen. "Come closer so we may talk."

Snoot climbed upon one of the carved granite chairs and then hopped on the table. He stood for a moment at the opposite end of the table, Father Screen's red eyes unwavering on his tiny frame.

"Closer," he said.

Snoot took a tiny step.

"Closer still," whispered Father Screen. "I warn you my patience is running thin. Come closer."

Snoot closed his eyes and took a few steps forward. The room was silent except for the ticking and churning of Father Screen's internal gears, and the ominous grumble of his molten-fire stomach. Snoot opened his eyes to find the large golden robot sitting directly before him.

Father Screen was a perfectly intact, golden version of Silo. The two would be identical had Silo not been so badly decayed.

"So I see that my brother is still alive. Looks like I'll have to put more resources into the water destruction system," said Father Screen.

"Yes, Sero," said Snoot.

"Don't consider knowing my real name a privilege. Any robot who has ever uttered it has been destroyed. Yes, I was once known as Sero, but Sero was horribly ugly, and I'm beautiful and golden. It would behoove you to call me Father Screen."

"And I'd prefer you call me a Lightbot," retorted Snoot.

Father Screen let out a monstrous laugh.

"Well, aren't you a brave little robot? A moment ago you wouldn't walk across this table," he mocked. "I could crush you in an instant. Remember that."

Snoot did not budge.

Father Screen sat silently for a moment, his red eyes intent on Snoot's iron frame. "Tell me, Snoot, I'm curious. Why did you come back?"

"I want to tell the Drudgebots what I know. I wanted to tell them you are tricking them into thinking they are free," said Snoot.

"Do you think I'd be foolish enough to believe that? We both know the Drudges would never listen to you. They would laugh at you like they always have. They listen to me. They believe me. It doesn't matter what I say or what visions I show, their hearts and minds are immersed in what I tell them. You came back to tell the Drudges the truth? Let us try again."

Snoot looked at the screens which were displaying images of his discoveries in RUR's chamber.

"I see everything that happens in the Dome, Snoot. I knew the moment you went outside and the moment you returned. You cannot hide from me. Nobody can. Only outside the Dome can you escape my eyes."

Snoot remained silent.

"If I were a robot in your position, my brain would have to be badly malfunctioning to come back to the Dome—especially to Halo City. Unless, of course, there was something I wanted. Something so precious that I'd risk my life to have it," said Father Screen. "My brother sent you back for the Orb, didn't he?"

The embers in his belly grew white-hot.

"Does he have the Shard? Did he send you back to steal the Orb?" roared Father Screen. "It doesn't matter where it is. If we don't find it in the mines, I'll find it in the scrap once it's rusted away. Does he still think he has power over me?" Father Screen smashed his fist to the granite table, almost hitting Snoot.

"You know where it is. He told you, didn't he?"

"No. I don't know where it is," said Snoot.

"You're lying."

Father Screen grabbed Snoot by his solar wings and held him at eye level. Snoot dangled feebly in his grasp.

"Drudge, tell me where it is, or I will ship you below to the mines, and the guards will strip your memory. I could see everything you've ever seen. Although, it is a terribly messy process and not foolproof."

He set Snoot upon the table.

"Drudge, I don't think you understand what you're up against. You have two choices: help me or be destroyed."

Father Screen looked to the ceiling for a long moment. In his eyes reflected a deep, undying anger, and the flames in his belly roared.

"You have no idea how it feels to be a slave and starved and told you are nothing. Or perhaps you do? I was once ugly like you. I remember what it's like and once I escaped, I swore I'd never cower or answer to anyone again—not to slave masters, not to the Maker Council, and certainly not to my brother. I am the most powerful robot this colony has ever seen, and one day very soon, my slaves will find the Shard and I will unite it with the Orb. Then nothing can stop me." Father Screen lowered his voice. "My beautiful face will be on every screen in the Universe, and I will reign over everything."

Father Screen was pleased. He focused his gaze upon Snoot, grabbed a handful of gold and iron ore from a pile next to his chair, and devoured it in one large gulp. Thick black oil dripped from the corners of his mouth, and a satisfied scarlet glow emitted from his belly.

"Absolutely delicious. Much better than the scrap old Silo feeds on, I'm sure."

He turned to Snoot, his eyes alive with excitement.

"Although part of me wants to swallow you whole, I think your gumption deserves a little reward, don't you? Golden Halo armor, or a Halo body, perhaps. So how about this? You tell me where Silo hid the Shard, and I'll give you your most cherished wish."

"I'll never tell."

Father Screen smirked.

"Hmm. Before you didn't know, and now you'll never tell. Which means you have seen it."

Snoot stood silently on the table—he thought of running, but knew Father Screen would crush him on the spot.

"One of the great joys I get in life is the amount of control I have over other robots' lives. I control each and every one of them; every robot has a price, you know. For the Drudges, it's enough light rations to power their shoddy rocket shoes and tacky golden bolts. The Halos are a bit pricey, but I control them too. You are different." He smiled, and the embers from his blast furnace lit the room. Large plumes of smoke and fire bellowed from his mouth. "How about you Snoot, what's your price?"

Father Screen's granite chair swiveled away from the table, and he faced the giant screen. Snoot thought about making a dash for the hoverlift, but knew he wouldn't get very far.

"Let's see, what am I to do with little Snoot, the bravest of all the Drudgebots? Hmm, I could smash him to bits or have his memory stripped. Maybe I will do both."

Father Screen paused, and his echo rang throughout the chamber.

"Better yet, I could have him rewired and turned into a Slavebot. I'd leave his little memory intact so he could sit plugged into the cylinder for an eternity, and think about how he's nothing more than a tool to make my life better. I like that."

"Or . . ." Father Screen stopped. His voice echoed heavily along the stone walls.

With one giant sweeping motion, Father Screen swiveled around in his chair and shoved his face before Snoot. He was mere centimeters away. Snoot could smell the sulfur and ash from Father Screen's mouth, and he stepped back a few paces.

"Or I could make a very special arrangement. You see, Snoot, in addition to collecting computations for the light, we can also collect the Drudges' innermost thoughts: their fears, desires, and dreams."

Father Screen sat back in his chair, and the reflection of the screens danced in his eyes. He lifted his left hand slowly and held a thin shard of glass between his thumb and forefinger. As he inserted the glass into a slot on the table, the screens surrounding the room lit up.

"I seem to recall a daydream of yours, Snoot, one I could easily make true. Just think about it, the robot they all picked on, the one they laughed at for his ugly tin bolts and sad demeanor. While the Drudges are sitting at the cylinder, that little robot appears next to RUR on the big screen—he's now the savior of Dome City. It turns out that he didn't steal any light, and that when he was banished from the Dome, he rebuilt himself and fought the Gremborgs single-handedly. Now he returns to his peers with a body of gold. He's shiny and revered by all. Snoot, you'd be the next RUR."

Father Screen smiled. He touched the pads of his fingers together, placed them against his chin, and stared intently at Snoot. "What's it going to be, Drudge?"

Snoot stared intently at his daydream displayed on the screens. He was so engrossed by it that he sat down upon the table, too weak to stand. The screens displayed images of Snoot polished, shiny, and rebuilt with golden armor; he was even taller. The Drudgebots lifted him high into the air, and declared him a hero. Snoot gazed upon the screen, and he longed to be that robot.

The Drudgebots carried him on their shoulders, and his golden armor outshined

everything in sight. All the Drudges shouted his name—they'd forgotten RUR.

And then something very strange caught his eye. Staring at his fantasy, Snoot noticed a very big smile upon his onscreen face. Snoot hadn't smiled in a long time.

"It's fake," whispered Snoot.

"Yes. But I could make it real. You'd never have to do another computation again."

"It'll still be fake, just like RUR. Just like everything."

"Little robot, I'm giving you the opportunity of a lifetime," growled Father Screen as plumes of smoke rose from his oil-smeared mouth.

"No. I don't want it."

Snoot turned to Father Screen and stared into his red eyes.

Father Screen was ghastly silent; the noise of his gears and motors echoed through the quiet chamber.

"My brother's a very clever robot, wouldn't you agree?" asked Father Screen. His voice was calm.

Snoot did not respond.

"Something just occurred to me," said Father Screen. "A master creator like Silo would never waste his time on building such a useless, ugly robot like you—unless there was a purpose."

Snoot took a few steps backward.

"There's really no purpose for a sickening robot like you to exist. So I have to ask myself, 'Why would Silo waste his precious time to create a walking pile of scrap?' There's no reason for it. No reason except . . ."

Father Screen smashed his fist upon the table, nearly crushing Snoot. Snoot backed away slowly.

Father Screen slowly opened his fist to reveal a metallic green ball. It looked like green mercury encased in shiny, clear glass, and it was a little larger than Snoot.

Snoot looked at the lifeless Orb and could see his reflection in it. He looked like he always did, but a bit fatter due to the curved surface of the Orb. But there was something else—something strange.

As Snoot looked to his torso, he saw an intense white-green glow pouring from his chest. He wasn't the only one who noticed.

The Orb was no longer dull. It was hovering above the table, glowing with a blinding green light.

"I knew it! It's in you!"

Father Screen's large hand hastily grabbed for Snoot, but his clumsiness sent Snoot flying from the table. The Orb came crashing down, again lightless, and Father Screen quickly grabbed it. He secured it in a compartment on his shoulder, and rose slowly, the gears in his body made a menacing creaking sound.

Father Screen walked to the other side of the table, and saw nothing but a bare floor. He knelt beside the table and peered underneath. Snoot was nowhere to be found.

"Snoot. Come on out, little one." His voice was gentle. "I'm sorry I yelled at you. You have no need to be frightened of me. I merely want the Shard. If you give it to me, I'll share some of the power with you, and we can rule together. You are a very special little robot, and I see that now."

Snoot remained still.

"Snoot, there is no escape from this room. There are Guards right outside the door, and you cannot make it to the hoverlift."

Father Screen walked to the opening that led to the hoverlift and he blocked the corridor.

"Come out, Snoot. You're time is up." Father Screen's voice was as heavy as mercury.

Snoot, hidden in the far corner of the room, watched from the shadows. Noticing the gap between Father Screen's legs was big enough for him to fit through, he dashed for the opening.

Father Screen tried to grab the little robot, but Snoot was too quick for him. Snoot slid freely through Father Screen's legs. Father Screen turned to follow Snoot, but the little Drudgebot was nowhere in sight.

"Guards!" howled Father Screen. Immediately two Guard commanders rushed in from the opposite entrance.

"Yes, sir," they said in unison.

"That pest has the Shard inside of him. He's escaped. I don't see him on any of my screens, but he could not have gotten far. Find that robot. He cannot escape."

The Guards ran past Father Screen, down the corridor, and hopped on the hover platform.

Father Screen turned and entered the corridor, not noticing that something very strange was attached to the back of his giant, golden leg. Or rather, something very familiar was clinging to the back of his leg: a small iron parasite Father Screen was too distracted to notice. Snoot held on for dear life as Father Screen thundered down the corridor. The moment Father Screen made it to the elevator shaft, Snoot let go and ran in the opposite direction.

"Down," commanded Father Screen. As the door to the shaft closed, he noticed Snoot's tiny frame racing to the end of the corridor.

Chapter 11. Escape

S noot ran to the opposite door, and it opened automatically. His feet had never traveled so quickly. As he scurried down the well-lit, pristine corridor, optical lenses dropped from the ceiling and traced his path. Father Screen knew exactly where Snoot was. White lights flashed to red and a deafening alarm echoed through the corridor.

Upon exiting, Snoot found himself on another walkway encircling Halo City. This walkway was much wider. He ran to the railing and peered over the side. Snoot was no longer peering into the heart of Halo City—he was in the very heart of it.

Hoversleds whizzed by him from wall to wall and up and down the bottomless drop. Even though he was deeper into Halo City, he still couldn't see the bottom. Directly in front of Snoot was a metal walkway that extended to the center of the golden well. It was a hoversled port.

"Stop!" yelled a Guard.

A large group of Guards quickly approached from Snoot's left. He turned to run, but a larger group of Halobots was closing in from his right. He had nowhere to go except the hoversled platform.

Snoot ran to the hoversled port and rounded the large cylindrical building at the platform's center. Upon reaching the opposite side, Snoot saw he had nowhere to run except a dead end that extended from the main platform. Trapped again! Snoot ran to the dead end's railing, and awaited the pursuing robots. Knowing they wanted the Shard, Snoot decided they'd get it.

As the Guards and Halos rounded both sides of the walkway, they saw Snoot's upper body leaning over the railing, his hands extended outward. In his grasp emitted a greenish glow.

"I'll drop it!" cried Snoot.

The pursuing robots stopped at the mouth of the dead end.

"I'll drop it down this hole, and you'll never find it. Don't come any closer."

The Guards immediately began to chatter amongst themselves to decide what to do. The Halos did the same. Several hoversleds lowered to Snoot's position. They swarmed above and below

him like a group of angry hummingbirds.

"Please drop it. Please do!"

Snoot peered to his right to notice Father Screen's figure emerge from behind the Halobots.

"It will be found," said Father Screen confidently.

A hoversled piloted by a lone Guardbot slid into position below Snoot. He was prepared to catch the Shard if Snoot dropped it.

Father Screen pushed his way to the front of his minions and confronted Snoot.

"Little Drudge, give us the Shard. There is nowhere for you to go."

Father Screen stepped slowly toward Snoot. He didn't want to upset the tiny robot and spend another eternity mining for the Shard in the depths below. Snoot decided it was best to quit his high balancing act and face Father Screen. His grasp was still tight around the Shard as he walked toward the massive, golden robot.

"Is this what you want?" Snoot tried to sound as bold as possible but his voice was nervous.

Father Screen advanced and so did Snoot. The two were very close. Father Screen's portly frame dwarfed the little robot, and his red eyes stared angrily at Snoot.

"Then come and get it!" cried Snoot.

Father Screen ran toward Snoot as quickly as his giant body would carry him.

"Give me the Shard!" he screamed.

Snoot ran for the railing—Father Screen was gaining quickly. As he reached the edge, Snoot threw the object over the side and dodged Father Screen's stampeding feet. So intent on the Shard was Father Screen that he crashed through the railing and dove for the glowing treasure. From the Guards' position on the platform, Father Screen's gargantuan body could be seen trailing a greenish glow into the dark depths of Halo City.

The Guards and the Halobots ignited their rocket shoes and quickly descended to chase Father Screen.

Snoot stood up and ran to the platform's mangled railing. He peered over the side and noticed the hoversled directly below him was empty. Snoot jumped over the railing and landed safely on the sled. He'd never been on a hoversled, let alone piloted one. On the controls were two simple levers. Snoot pushed the one on the right, and the craft launched forward. He pulled it, and the craft crept backward. Realizing the other lever must be the vertical controls, Snoot pushed it, and the craft shot upward. As he zipped passed the platform, he saw Sorn motioning to some surrounding Guards. They immediately shot into the air, pursuing Snoot.

Snoot reached Halo City's ceiling, and the elevator to Dome City extended downward to greet him. The Guards were gaining fast. Snoot guided the craft until it met the descended elevator. As Snoot entered the elevator, he slammed the hoversled's vertical controls downward sending it on a perilous and uncontrolled descent into the pursuing Guards. Snoot commanded the lift upward, and once again stood in the heart of Dome City.

The Guards chasing Father Screen found his body smashed to oblivion at the bottom of the mining shaft. A pool of molten lava from his stomach was rapidly melting Father Screen into golden liquid. Nothing, not even a Makerbot, could have put him back together. The only part of Father Screen left intact was his large golden fist. It was clenched tightly, and a faint green glow emitted from the cracks in between his fingers.

"There! His fist. He caught the Shard," announced a Guard commander.

Several Guardbots moved in and forced open Father Screen's dead hand. It creaked and moaned as they pried it open. When they finally opened his massive fist and peered into his golden palm, they found not the Shard, but a perfectly intact glowing, green apple.

Chapter 12. Back from the Dead

noot stood at the base of the cylinder.

"Everyone! Everyone! We have to leave the Dome! They're going to melt us down!" Snoot jumped up and down waving his arms to get the attention of the busy Drudgebots. Shocked to see Snoot alive and well, they unplugged themselves and rushed to the Dome floor.

Due to the commotion below in Halo City, there was only one Guardbot on duty at the cylinder, and very few Halobots lounging about on the encircling walkways. The Guard on duty walked calmly toward Snoot. A sea of Drudgebots surrounded him.

"What's this, little one? What's all the commotion about?" asked the Guard pleasantly—always smiling.

"Listen everyone, we've got to leave the Dome! Father Screen is going to melt us down."

On any other day, none of the Drudgebots would have believed Snoot, but to see a robot back from the dead had them thinking differently.

"How do you know that, Snoot?" asked a Drudgebot.

"Now, now, Drudgebots, return to your sockets. This one is obviously malfunctioning and not worth the wasted work time. Father Screen and the Halobots love you—I can assure you of that."

As the Guardbot was trying to silence any doubts the Drudges might have, something very strange was happening on the screens above. Father Screen was lying dead many kilometers below the Dome floor and no longer controlled the screens. They were flashing static and random images. And then, Father Screen's face appeared.

"I was once ugly like you . . ." His voice boomed throughout Dome City.

Father Screen's image flashed off and on, and the Drudgebots turned their attention to the massive screens. An image of Snoot standing before Father Screen flickered off and on. The screen went dark and slowly came to life with a projection of Father Screen sitting around the table of Halobots.

"I'm tired of wasting light on those putrid Drudgebots . . ."

A sullen hush swept the crowd.

"That light can be used to make our lives more luxurious!"

The screens blipped again and flashed to Father Screen standing around the table of Halobots.

"I want those Drudgebots melted down for parts as soon as you can do it," said Father Screen. The screens flickered between his face and static, and his words repeated over and over.

"I want those Drudgebots melted down for parts . . ."

The screens fell to blackness and the crowd gasped.

"Now, now, Drudges. I'm sure this is just a hoax," said the Guard calmly. His hand reached for his shock stick.

"Listen everyone, we're doomed if we stay here. We must escape the Dome. I know someone who can help," interjected Snoot.

"We can't leave the Dome! There's nothing beyond, and the Gremborgs will eat us alive," panicked a Drudgebot.

"Listen to me! I've been outside. I know a safe place. I think we might be able to find light. If we stay here, we're doomed," cried Snoot.

The Guard, tired of Snoot's ramblings and nervous due to being outnumbered nearly five hundred to one, jammed his shock stick into Snoot's shoulder and sent him reeling to the floor.

"Hey!" yelled Twiggy. "That's my buddy."

The Drudgebots swarmed around the Guard and began beating him with their bronze fists. He was able to fend them off for a few seconds, but he was greatly outnumbered. The Guard ran as quickly as he could for the elevator to Halo City.

"Snoot, how do you know we can live outside the Dome?" asked Twiggy.

"I don't, but I know someone who might be able to help. If we stay here, we'll be killed. We have to take the chance. I know a safe place."

"I believe him. He's been outside, and has come back."

The crowd turned to A2.

"He showed me something from outside. I'm going with Snoot," she said.

"Me too, little buddy! Lead the way," encouraged Twiggy.

"But what about the Gremborgs?" asked a Drudge.

"They're not really Gremborgs," began Snoot. "I know the robot who controls them—I'll explain everything later, but if you're quiet and follow my lead, we can make it to safety."

Snoot herded the Drudgebots to the trash conveyor. He entered the security code and opened the exit door.

Snoot stayed at the mouth of the opening guiding each Drudge down the mountain of scrap. His tiny voice could be heard shouting encouraging words to the descending Drudges. Soon, all but the skeptical Drudges were outside. Snoot was the last to climb down.

The misting machines created a thick fog that hovered over the scrapyard. Snoot ran to the entrance of Silo's chamber, but found the opening had caved in. Snoot needed help—fast.

He climbed upon the scrap mountain and yelled to the Drudges below.

"OK, listen, everyone. I'm going to guide you out of the scrapyard, but you have to be very careful and follow my steps. Don't get caught in the open or the mist will cling to your armor and you will rust. Stick very close to the sidewalls, and it'll give you shelter. Just do what I do, and you will be fine."

He knew if anyone could help, it had to be Fernando. When Snoot and the others arrived at the apple tree, they found Tik and Tak sobbing at its base.

"Tik, Tak, what's wrong?" asked Snoot.

"Oh, our metal friend. It's so good to see you," wept Tak.

Tak dried his tears for a moment and flew to greet Snoot.

"It's our Fernando. He's dead! He's buried inside that strange tomb that hangs next to his apple."

Snoot looked to the tree and noticed a strange object hanging next to Fernando's apple.

"Our good friend's gone, yes, look and see.

His tomb hangs from the apple tree," said Tik.

"He was so young, so healthy," replied Tak.

Tak continued to weep miserably. Snoot's legs weakened, and he sat to look at the strange tomb. "Fernando?" he whispered. There was no answer.

"Fernando is dead," moaned Tak. He flew to rest his head on Snoot's shoulder. Tik landed gently upon Snoot's head for comfort.

A2 walked to Snoot and placed her hand upon Snoot's back.

"Snoot, what's going on? The Drudges and I are worried. We've come too far from the Dome to make it back on our batteries. Where's the light you promised? This darkness is scaring us."

"I don't know, A2. I wanted to ask the caterpillar. I knew he'd have an answer but he's dead. I've failed you. I've failed everyone."

Snoot had led the Drudgebots to certain doom. To make things worse, he knew Sorn and the Guardbots would soon surface to hunt for the Shard and arrest the escaped Drudges. They'd all be melted down. Snoot was out of ideas and out of time. He looked to his chest and pulled out the Shard. It's green light seemed no brighter than the light shining from Tik and Tak.

And then something clicked inside his mechanical brain.

Snoot stood and ran toward the scrapyard.

"Snoot, where are you going?" shouted A2.

"I've got an idea. Wait here," he shouted as he disappeared into darkness.

Chapter 13. Terribly Tasty

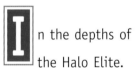n the depths of Halo City, Sorn was meeting in Father Screen's chamber with the Halo Elite.

"Is the Orb secured?" asked a commanding Halobot.

"Yes, sir," said Sorn.

"Good. Place it in my chamber, I am now the keeper of the Orb."

"I want the Shard immediately!" the Halobot continued, "Father Screen is dead and I am in control. Sorn, gather your best Guards. Surface to the scrapyard; find the Shard, and bring back every single one of those worthless Drudgebots!"

"Sir, the mist will rust us before we can find them," warned Sorn. "Without Father

Screen, we can't execute the command to shut it off."

"Rust does not concern me, Sorn. Do as I say."

One hundred of Sorn's most fearsome Guards soon exited the Dome and entered the scrapyard.

"Scan the yard for any signs of movement—it's the little one we're after. Act quickly or we'll be too rusted to move."

The Guards stood for a moment, scanning the various corridors of the scrapyard.

"Sir, I see him," announced one of the Guards.

Sorn led them down the pathway. As they got closer to Snoot's position, they could see the green glow of the Shard in his chest. The light immediately zipped off to the right, and the Guards followed. From behind them, a voice beckoned, "Here I am!"

The Guards turned toward the voice. The fog was heavy through the maze-like pathways, but they could see the green light coming from Snoot. Yet the second the Guards reached Snoot's position, he had zipped down another corridor.

The mist was starting to rust the Guards' armor and they were moving more slowly. As they followed Snoot deeper into the scrap mazes, they became terribly confused. Snoot seemed to be everywhere at once. One moment he was in front of them, the next he would appear behind them, taunting them as they tracked him deeper into the scrap maze.

"I'm here," beckoned his little voice.

They'd turn to chase the light and suddenly—"I'm behind you!" he'd shout.

The Guards panicked.

"We need to find shelter," shouted one of the Guards.

"It's best if we find him from the sky. Ignite your rocket shoes!" commanded Sorn.

The Guards tried to ignite their rocket shoes, but they were too wet to work.

"There he is. Follow that light."

The Guards followed Snoot into an opening in the mounds of scrap and down into a dark cave. It was a dead end.

"You're trapped, Snoot. Surrender at once," shouted Sorn.

The green light didn't budge.

"I shall duel to the death, you wicked tyrant!" asserted the voice.

"Grab him!" shouted Sorn.

Sorn and one hundred of his finest Guardbots dashed toward Snoot. They lunged at him from every direction, yet he was too quick. It finally dawned on the Guards that the green light had no body when it shot into the air and split in two. The two specks of green light hovered above them.

"Ha! Ha! You fools!" said Tak as he danced above their heads.

"Silly Guards, you have no mind.

The Shard you seek, but will not find!" heckled Tik.

Tik and Tak swooped out of the cave, and the Guards turned to chase them. They didn't get far. The corrosive mist had completely eaten away at their joints. Some of the Guards were frozen in place; others fell to the ground as their knee joints split apart.

"It's OK!" shouted Sorn. "I'll signal for help."

"There will be no signaling for help, little Tastys," spoke a crackling voice.

"Who said that?" yelled Sorn.

The guards looked around the dim room but didn't see anything.

"So yummy. So yummy," taunted another voice.

"I order you to show yourself," demanded Sorn. He frantically dug his fingers into the ground and slithered toward the exit. After a few desperate pulls, his fingers ripped from his hands, too decayed to withstand the weight of his body.

"Sir, what if it's Gremborgs?"

"Don't be stupid. Gremborgs don't exist," said Sorn.

Meanwhile, the walls moved.

"What's that?" yelled a guard on the floor.

The rest of the guards watched in horror as two enormous robots emerged from the chamber walls. Ravin's hulking frame dipped slowly from the ceiling and Morter emerged from the far wall. The red glow from their blast furnace stomachs lit the room as they hulked over their immobilized prey.

"So yummy. So yummy," hissed Ravin.

"Tasty dinner is served," spoke Morter.

Tik and Tak flew as quickly as they could from the scrapyard. Piercing metallic screams and terrible crunching sounds echoed behind them; and then—silence.

Chapter 14. It's Always Darkest

he Halo Elite sat at the table waiting intently for news from the surface. A Guard rushed into the room.

"Sir, we've lost contact with Sorn," he said.

"Well, try another Guard," said the commander.

"That's just it, sir. We've lost contact with all the Guards. They seem to have been destroyed."

The room was gravely silent.

"One hundred of your finest Guards destroyed by a meter-tall robot?" he asked.

"Sir, the Life Light is dimming—we're running out of power."

The Halo commander turned to the Guard, and as he began to speak, the room fell to blackness.

Tik and Tak reached the apple tree to find Snoot seated with the rest of the Drudgebots.

"Taadaaaa!" yelled Tak as he landed in front of Snoot. "What did I say? You just wait here, and we'd take care of those Guards!"

Snoot didn't respond.

"I told you those Guards were no match for the dreaded General Tak. They are now resting in the belly of those foul machines that scour the yard." Tak was shocked at Snoot's lack of gratitude.

"What's wrong, Snoot? You're free now. They'll never come looking for a robot who can defeat one hundred Guards."

Snoot slowly lifted his head. "I'm dying, Tak. Some of the others are already gone," said Snoot. "There's nothing left for me. I've failed."

A moment later, Snoot's battery alarm beeped and he knew it wouldn't be much longer until his power was gone. He'd be another piece of lifeless scrap sitting on the asteroid. Even if he wanted to, he didn't have enough power to make it back to the Dome.

"Oh, no! Not you too. Little Snoot, you can't die. You're our friend," moaned Tak.

The green light emitted by the fireflies grew dim in Snoot's eyes, and his senses began to numb.

Snoot barely had enough energy to speak. His voice was very deep and slurry. "I can't live without light. I need light or my battery dies."

"Snoot, just wait throughout the night,

and then . . ."

Tik's words floated softly to Snoot's audio sensors and died off before Snoot could hear what she had to say. Snoot's world grew dark. His last vision was of the firefly light shrinking into a small, dim, green speck. The speck soon died out and so did Snoot. He and the rest of the Drudgebots sat like metal skeletons, motionless. They died free robots.

Tik and Tak jumped to flight as Snoot's body slumped over. He was completely limp, and not a whir or a blip did his tiny body make. Snoot was no more. The two fireflies hovered above his head, not knowing what to do.

The Orb was many kilometers below the asteroid surface, and the Shard would remain safely hidden within Snoot. The two would never be reunited. Snoot died a hero's death. The fireflies' green light cast a stark, eerie glow upon Snoot's lifeless metal body, and if you looked close enough, you could see on his little robot face a very real smile.

THE END

CHAPTER 15. HAPPY ROBOTS

Well, to say THE END is a bit pessimistic.

It was definitely the end for the Halobots. At the rate they consumed light, the entirety of Halo City soon fell into utter darkness. The Halos and Guards, unable to produce for themselves, ran out of power and grew lost and confused in the darkness.

And what of little Snoot and the rest of the Drudgebots? Well, it turns out that if a robot follows his heart, light can be found in the strangest of places. You see, there was a very big secret Father Screen kept only to himself—something he worked very hard to ensure the Drudgebots, the Guardbots and even the Halobots would never learn of.

Though it seemed like the Dome was the only source of light, and though it seemed like there was only darkness and cold outside; every morning—at the same time as the morning before and the morning before that—a sun rises outside of the Dome. Yes, a sun—a big, glorious, yellow sun brimming with life and energy. Living a life plugged into the cylinder, no robot ever imagined a light brighter than the Life Light existed, especially just outside the Dome's thin walls.

Snoot had never heard of the sun until he awoke that dawn to feel his circuits warmed in a way he never before experienced. He looked into the sky and shielded his eyes from the blistering sunlight. He opened and closed his fists to make sure he wasn't imagining things. His entire body felt wonderful. In the distance he could see the Dome. It looked like nothing more than an upside-down, dull, white bowl. The mist machines stopped after the Dome ran out of power, and the scrapyard appeared as carelessly tossed reddish brown wreckage. It encircled the Dome for as far as Snoot could see. The junk was more gnarled and twisted than Snoot imagined, and he wondered how he was able to navigate through such a mess in the darkness. He thought of Silo, and wondered why the giant robot didn't mention this glorious light outside the Dome. Snoot hoped they'd meet again one day so he could ask.

Snoot stood up and saw his fellow Lightbots awakening.

"Snoot, you did it!" yelled a voice.

He turned to see Twiggy running toward him. "You did it, little buddy! Where'd you get all this light?"

A2 ran to Snoot and embraced him. "I knew you could do it, Snoot! I'm sorry for ever doubting you."

The other Lightbots ran to Snoot and picked him high into the air. They carried him about on their shoulders, and cheered his name.

"Come on, Snoot! Tell us, where you get all this light? It feels so good," said a Lightbot.

"The truth is, I don't know," answered Snoot.

The Lightbots declared him a hero; everyone wanted to shake his hand.

A very familiar voice came from above. "Hello there, Snoot! How's the sunlight treating you?"

Snoot looked up to see Fernando fluttering above him.

"Fernando?" asked Snoot.

Fernando was no longer a green caterpillar but a magnificent butterfly. His wings swooped gracefully to keep his brown body afloat. Fernando shadowed Snoot's eyes from the piercing sunlight, and his wings shone like a velveteen rainbow. Snoot was dazzled by the array of colors in Fernando's wings—blue tones and green hues and circles of yellow and arrays of